HONORABLE DARKNESS

The Story of Hex & Snip

The Realm Series

Honorable Darkness
The Story of Hex & Snip

The Realm Series

C. R. Rice

4 Horsemen
Publications, Inc.

DEDICATION

For Zayn,
... and beyond

Table of Contents

Chapter One

The Realm was on fire.

Buildings were crumbling, and the blare of relentless explosions brought a constant uncomfortable buzz to Callen's eardrums. Bodies littered the cracked and blackened streets. Ash rained down like snow, leaving the air heavy with the putrid smell of death and destruction. The screams had ended hours ago, replaced only with faint moans, groans, and the pleading words of those begging for death.

Callen peered around a smoldering building, his eyes molten. "Move!" he hissed.

A small, dirty, and limping group pushed from the war-washed building and, with hunched bodies, crossed the battle-ridden street. As he followed, Callen kept his head on a swivel, his eyes seeing deeper than ever before. The world lay bare before his gaze, broken into infinite layers. He saw everything: beams that threatened to break, bodies trapped beneath rubble, intruders sneaking on the tips of their toes as they wove in and out of the shadows.

Orion was the first to reach the other side. Glass crunched beneath his feet as he inched closer to the dented door. Holding his breath, he reached a tentative hand forward and prayed to any surviving gods that the door was unlocked. The knob twisted and his breath left in a rush. Orion pulled the door wide, kicking aside the fallen remnants of a stripped pink awning with his steel-toed boot.

"Everyone in," he ordered.

One by one, the injured and weary streamed inside. Despite the promise of shelter, they remained on high alert. Anything could happen. Magic and swords were no longer the only weapons in this new, unknown world. There was more to fear than the burn of magic and sting of the blade.

Radnar lifted his sword and entered first, his hand clasped tightly around Agnes's as his eyes swept the darkened interior. Hex was tight on their heels, dragging his limping brother behind him. Callen walked backward to the building, his eyes continuing their sweep until Orion rested a hand on his shoulder. Together, the pair turned in and shut the door solidly, yet silently, behind them. Callen clenched his hands at his sides before drawing them up in a swift X. Instantly, earth speared the air in large, thick spikes, reinforcing the door.

"Clear," Radnar called.

Callen tipped his head in appreciation as he moved to the back door and the large window, repeating his reinforcing technique.

Radnar sheathed his sword and took Agnes into his arms. "Are you alright?"

The woman nodded as tears tracked through the muck and grime covering her face. "It can't be true," she cried, burying her face in his chest.

Radnar ran his hands up and down her trembling back. "It's going to be alright," he cooed. "This isn't the end. Not by a long shot."

Hex shifted his hold on his brother, tightening his grip on Snip's bloodied waist as he led them across the room. "This is going to hurt," Hex warned.

Snip chuckled. "That's what she said."

Hex paused, confused. "What did *who* say?"

Snip waved a clumsy hand. "Nothing, something Thane said the—"

"Let me help you," Orion interjected, rushing to Snip's other side to help Hex guide him to the ground.

Snip groaned as they dropped him on the hard surface. "Stars! *Throw* me next time. It'll be less painful."

Hex rolled his eyes and kicked a broken chair from his path. "I warned you it would hurt." He continued to move around the room, following Callen's path from door to window. His lips moved in a blur as his eyes darkened. He lifted his hands and a thick, ink-like substance oozed from his fingertips to puddle on the floor. The group watched in a mixture of awe and disgust as the substance slithered along the floor, rising to cover Callen's spiked barricade. The thick liquid shifted, twisting into ancient runes before dissolving into the stone.

Orion suppressed a disgusted shiver and crouched down to look Snip in the eye. "Hey, buddy, how are you doing?"

Snip looked up with a smile. "You called me 'buddy.'" His smile faded and eyes widened as he watched Hex whisper with Callen. "Oh stars, you called me 'buddy.' I'm dying, aren't I? Oh, stars, I'm *dying*!"

All eyes shifted to Snip as his dramatics grew in intensity. "Shut up, you idiot!" Orion snapped. "You are not dying. I was trying to be nice!"

"Oh, Crixus, Ori's being nice. Ori's being nice! It's true! I *am* dying." Snip lifted a hand to his chest and looked for his brother. "Hex, my beloved brother. My twin, my less attractive, humorless other half! I lied. It *was* me that drank all of your fancy glowing wine and spilled that weird green goo all over your old books, not Ori."

Orion jerked. "Seriously? What the hell, Snip? Do you know what he did to me for that?"

Hex shook his head. "I knew it," he whispered to Callen.

Rocks shifted beneath Snip as he turned to Callen. An errant rock jabbed him in the back, pulling a pained groan from his lips. "Oh Allie, aw buddy. I'm sorry for the cupcakes. I lied, I knew what they were, and I thought it would be funny."

4

Callen shook his head, crossing his arms over his broad chest. "You have no honor."

Snip waved a hand in Orion's direction. "But Ori was there. He knew. The man should have stopped me. He knows, just as all best—"

"We are not best friends."

"—*best* friends do. I have no self-control."

Orion shook his head as he shoved from Snip's side and rose. "What the Fornax, Snip? Will someone shut him up?"

"I have been trying since birth, and I have yet to find a way," Hex remarked.

Snip sighed. "I'm sorry Ori, but a man must be honest when on his deathbed."

"You're not dying, you idiot!" Orion seethed. Slowly, he turned to face Callen's disapproving stare. "Sorry about the cupcakes."

Callen just shook his head disapprovingly.

"If it helps, we had just finished our fifth bottle of ogre ale and would have never done it otherwise," Orion added, rocking back on his heels.

Callen pursed his lips as he considered the man's words. "It does not."

Orion blew out a breath and shrugged. "I tried."

"And Radnar," Snip continued.

Radnar lifted a brow, his hands halting their soothing ministrations against Agnes's back as he prepared himself for the words to come.

"Ah, you salt-and-pepper fox, you." Snip hesitated, his mouth opening and closing several times before finally, he shook his head in resignation. "I can't say what I did to you, but I'm sure there's something."

Radnar chuckled as he led Agnes to a chair. "I have no doubt," he admitted. "Hex, can you look at Agnes? She has been favoring her right side since the blast."

"Of course, right after I fix this idiot." Hex rolled his shoulders, his eyes glowing as bright as freshly spilled blood as he approached his brother. "This is going to hurt," he promised.

"That should be your catchphrase. It's the most common thing you say-AH!" An unexpected explosion crashed outside their hideout, shaking the building and bringing stone crumbling down onto Snip's wounded leg.

In a flash, Hex was by his side, slapping a heavy hand over his brother's mouth. "Do you want to be found?" he hissed in his ear. "Callen and I can only do so much."

The room fell into uncertain silence as they awaited their fates.

Chapter Two

Uncertainty did strange things to time, like stretching it out into indefinite lengths as the weight of the unknown pressed down upon their unwilling souls. They held their breath as their pounding hearts raged against the confines of their ribcages. As they exchanged nervous looks, a mutual fear of the unknown glittered in their eyes.

Agnes lifted a trembling hand to her lips as a frightened sob threatened to break free. Radnar tightened his hold, giving her a reassuring squeeze as his eyes drifted from one enchanted seal to the next. Orion carefully pulled his gun free of its holster, the gold inlet shimmering in the dim light. Slowly, Hex rose to his feet while Callen leaned against the wall and stared at Snip, seemingly unphased by the turn of events. His eyes burned with a fierce light as he continued to stare at Snip.

The silence stretched on as they considered their next move. Would they be found? If so, by whom? A door rattled and Agnes's sob escaped. Her eyes pinched tightly shut, forcing a tear to fall. Radnar freed his sword from its sheath and carefully maneuvered Agnes behind his back. Hex's eyes flashed with their crimson promise before swiftly darkening. His brow pinched in confusion.

A stillness filtered through the air a moment before blue light exploded in the dim, tiny room. A static buzz filled the room as lightning slapped the cracked linoleum, bringing dark, acrid smoke to the air.

Radnar spun toward Agnes, shielding her from the impending strikes. Hex rolled his eyes and Callen straightened, his teeth indenting his lower lip. Orion watched the display with morbid curiosity, his eyes bouncing from the chaotic display to Hex and Callen's relaxed stance.

With one last pop, the buzz of lightning ended, leaving the room filled with dust and black smoke. Snip coughed and waved his hand in front of his face to clear the air. "Stars, haven't you worked on your entrance?" he sputtered.

Radnar frowned as he uncurled from around Agnes's shivering body and directed his attention to the clearing smoke. The click of boots against linoleum echoed as two shadowed forms emerged from the smoke. The shorter figure wore spike-like protrusions above each shoulder while the other towered above him, imposing in both stature and width.

"Sorry we're late."

Radnar's frown deepened as the familiar voice registered. "Silas?"

Callen expelled a heavy breath, diminishing the weighted air. Instantly, the two figures were revealed. The two protrusions Radnar had thought were spikes on the smaller man's shoulders, were Silas's favored dual swords strapped to his back while the large, broad man was even more imposing than his shadow had suggested.

Silas grinned, revealing white teeth, his strange teal eyes twinkling with joy. "How have you been, old man?"

Radnar wrapped Silas in a tight embrace. "I thought you were dead."

Silas chuckled as the pair separated. "Nothing can take me down that easily. I just needed to recuperate."

Radnar shook his head, his eyes drifting to the other strange presence. The man stood with a stoic look on his face while his ashen eyes held a glittering intent as they drifted from person to person. His short, peppered hair was at odds with his youthful complexion. While his towering height and imposing width were enough to make anyone uncomfortable, the strange pulsing lines that ran the length of his arms and webbed his neck brought an uneasy pit to Radnar's stomach. *Something is off with that one.*

Silas met Callen's glowing stare. "Is it done?"

Callen nodded. Silas's eyes closed on a painful sigh before he, too, nodded. "Alright," he breathed.

Lifting a hand, he motioned to the solid form behind him. "This is Xander. He prefers X."

Callen stepped forward with narrowed eyes. "Forty-two?" he asked.

X tipped his head.

"He's Callen. That old grizzly looking one is Radnar—" Silas began to explain.

"Watch it, *boy*," Radnar growled.

Silas winked at the older man before continuing. "That's Agnes." Silas smiled and gave a small wave in her direction. "The one with the gun is Orion—"

"Ryan," Ryan corrected, his hand flexing on the cool steel pommel.

"Riiight." Silas dragged out the word before giving a dismissive flick of his wrist toward the twins. "And you know Snip and Hex."

X grunted, his enormous arms crossing over his chest. His eyes darkened as a growl began to rumble his chest.

Silas shook his head and thumped the man in the ribs. "Calm down," he muttered. "X here has some … *issues* we are working on."

Snip chuckled, the sound punctuated by a hiss as pain speared through his side. "That's putting it mildly." Leaning back against a cracked wall, he welcomed the pulsating pain from his injuries. If he could feel, he was still alive. His head fell forward, his vision unsteady, as he struggled to focus on the debris beneath his hands. Blood trickled down his forearm and dripped off his fingertips, splashing against the fallen brick.

A tap on his head had him opening eyes he hadn't realized he closed. Silas crouched in front of him, mirth dancing in his strange eyes. "Rough day?"

Hex chose that moment to grip his brother's head, his eyes going from crimson to pale rose in an instant. Silas lunged forward, covering the man's parted mouth with both hands as Snip's eyes filled with darkness.

Agnes's eyes went impossibly wide. "I don't need his help," she whispered into Radnar's ear.

The man chuckled as he leaned down to whisper, "He is not normally so rough. It's a brother thing."

X looked on with unveiled fascination as the sounds of snapping bones filled the air. Before their eyes, Snip's injuries were healing. Tendons slithered from the ghastly wound, wrapped around the loose, exposed muscle, and dragged it back into place with a sickening slurp. Skin stitched itself together, the porous pieces zipping together until nothing but blood-stained patches remained.

Hex removed his hands from his brother's scalp and crouched beside him. "The rest is up to you," he panted, his shoulder bumping Snip's as he brushed the blood from his own wounded cheek. The two were like magnets, whether repelling one another or joined at the hip when times grew dire. Brotherhood won.

After several moments, Hex nudged his brother once more. "Are you ready?" he asked.

Snip dropped his head back against the wall and shrugged. "Might as well, I suppose."

The group shifted before them, each taking an unconscious step forward as they looked at the pair with curious eyes.

Hex released a heavy breath before finally lifting his crimson gaze. "It's time we shared the truth of our past."

Chapter Three

"Your Highness! Your Highness, you must come quickly!"

Caelum was already on his feet and running when the door blew wide open. As the first frantic pleas left the frazzled maid's mouth, he broke into a run. He heard Lytos's worried shouts, but all he cared about was making it to his wife's side in time. By the time he crossed the threshold, his portal was already there. Another step through it and he stood in the softly lit medical chambers.

"Caelum," his wife's breathy voice beckoned.

He blinked several times to adjust his eyes to the sudden shift in the light. His wife lay in a bed of white, her face flushed and brow glistening with sweat. "Evelyn, my love, what is it? What's wrong?" He rushed to stand at her bedside.

Tears swam in her eyes, making them gleam like the jewels they were often compared to. "Nothing, my love. The baby is coming a little early, is all."

Caelum's eyes widened. The blood drained from his face and fear twisted his stomach. "The baby? *Now?* Are you sure?"

Evelyn's laugh was quickly severed by the sharp, unrelenting pain that sliced through her stomach. When it ebbed, she turned to her husband and nodded. "I am fairly certain."

Caelum smiled and took Evelyn's hand between his and kissed her fingers. "Let's greet our son."

What seemed like an agonized lifetime passed before they heard the baby's first triumphant cry. Evelyn fell back against the pillows with sweat tracing her brow. A mix of laughter and relief broke through her lips as the child was placed on her chest. The pink-skinned baby sported a thick crop of black hair that was slicked back with blood and a thick, white vernix. Never had the pair seen something so beautiful.

Evelyn kissed the baby's wet forehead as tears joined the sweat in rivers down her cheeks. The baby flailed in displeasure, his cries a sweet sound to his parent's ears. "Hello, little one," she cried. The doctor handed her a small cloth that she used to wipe the excess fluid from his tiny body as she softly cooed sweet nothings into his ear. The baby quieted at the familiar voice.

Evelyn looked up to Caelum and found him staring back with resplendent love. "He's beautiful," he breathed.

Evelyn beamed up at her husband. "He is, isn't he? Oh…"

Panic stilled Caelum's heart as he watched Evelyn's face fall into a mask of pain. "Evelyn? Evelyn, what is it? What's wrong?"

Evelyn shook her head, her breath trapped in her lungs. Her stomach tensed against the burn of pain. "I-I don't know."

"Doctor! Something is wrong!" Caelum called.

The doctor turned from the nearby table, his hands already glowing with a healing green light. "Take the child," he ordered.

His nurse moved to Evelyn's side and carefully took the sleeping child from her arms. "I will bring him right back," she promised.

Evelyn's painful cries were soon joined by that of her firstborn. The nurse rocked him gently and whispered sweet tales.

Caelum watched the doctor examine his wife with hawk-like eyes.

The moment the green faded from his fingertips, the doctor stood.

"Doctor?" Caelum asked.

The doctor stared at Evelyn in fear and shock, but there was something else too: a flicker of excitement. "She's… there's another one."

Caelum blinked. "Another what?"

The doctor frowned. "Another baby."

Caelum shook his head. "No, that's not possible. It's actually impossible."

The doctor shook his head and took his seat between Evelyn's legs. "I am afraid it is very possible, and we are all about to witness it. Your Majesty, I am going to need you to push."

Evelyn looked with terrified eyes at her husband. "Caelum," she whispered through the pain. "I can't do this. Not again."

Caelum cleared his throat and squeezed Evelyn's hand. "Yes, you can. Everything is going to be fine. You have created a miracle. Well, two miracles. Now push, love. Let's meet our impossible."

Bathed in her husband's powerful aura, Evelyn pushed, freeing the unexpected from her body. A second round of cries filled the air, matching the first. The doctor severed the tie connecting the baby to his mother and placed him on her chest.

"They are a perfect match," he whispered.

Caelum eyed the doctor as his overly interested tone twitched his ear. Slowly, Caelum rose to his feet, power leaking from his pores as he scowled at the man. "Hear me and hear me well, good *doctor*. If word of my children spreads from this room before I allow it, your life and that of those you love will be forfeit."

The doctor swallowed through the fear that clogged his throat and hastily nodded his head. "Of course, Your Highness. Never, Your Highness."

Evelyn looked from her newest bundle to her trembling husband as the twins let out a shrill cry.

"Caelum, my love, that is enough. No one would betray you in such a manner. These boys are a gift, not a curse, not an impossibility. They are ours."

Caelum speared the doctor with one last heated glare before returning to his seat and admiring his second born. "They really are a matching pair," he whispered in awe.

"Shall we bring them together and find out?" Evelyn giggled.

Caelum smiled at his wife and nodded. "Yes, we shall. Nurse, please bring him over." Sensing no movement, Caelum's smile began to fade as he glanced up and found the nurse staring at his family in horror.

"This is wrong. Blasphemy. The Stars would never have allowed it!" she screamed.

Caelum gritted his teeth against the desire to transport her to the pits of hell while she cradled one of his sons to her chest. "Give me my son." His voice was soft, calm, and oh so deadly.

The nurse frantically shook her head, a manic fire beginning to ignite in her eyes. "You cannot keep them a secret. The Realm deserves to know that the end is near!"

The woman moved like lightning and Caelum's stomach hit the floor. One moment, she stood in the corner, clutching his crying son. The next, his second son was pulled from his wife's arms and the door was blown open. She moved immeasurably fast while the babies squalled.

He was moving too slowly, his hands rising as if swimming in molasses. By the time he flicked his wrist, she was already dodging the newly opened portal. Bile burned his throat as her hand wrapped about the golden doorknob. A quick twist and she burst through the opened doorway … right into someone's waiting arms.

"What's going on here?"

Relief slammed against his chest with such force, Caelum hit his knees. "Lytos," he breathed.

Chapter Four

Lytos's smile lit the room with a joyous light. His grip tightened on the crazed woman as she attempted to twist from his grasp. He tipped his head and two of his men took their place at her sides. "Do you mind?" he asked.

Pinned beneath the full weight of his emerald gaze, the woman was transfixed, obblivious to anything but his stare. Lytos carefully extracted the squirming pair from her arms. Caelum crumpled to his knees, chest rising in deep breaths as his mind struggled to comprehend what had just happened. Evelyn's disbelieving whimpers sounded somewhere far away as a buzzing filled his ears.

Black shoe tips entered his eye line as a warm hand gripped his shoulder. "Is everything alright, Caelum?" Lytos asked.

Caelum's mouth opened and closed, like a fish gasping for water, before he finally shook his head.

"Up you go," Lytos chuckled, lifting his friend from the ground and setting him in the chair. "Everything is fine. See?"

Caelum shifted, a sob breaking free when he saw his wife cradling both sleeping boys. She gave him a tear-laced smile and squeezed the bundles tightly to her chest. His eyes fell on the copied pair. Their sleep-softened faces were pink with health, and they dozed with their fingers intertwined.

Lytos twirled his fingers as he stood next to Caelum and waited. As the seconds stretched into minutes, Lytos pursed his lips, a mischievous light glittering in his eyes. The tile bulged as the roots of a tree broke through and twisted into a woven chair, shrouded in flowers and leaves in every shade. Lytos smiled at the beauty and sat, content when the companionable silence continued to stretch between them.

"Not even five minutes into being a father and I already almost lost them."

"Oh, the joys of fatherhood." Lytos chuckled.

Caelum shook his head, his eyes still fixed on his family. "I'm serious, Lytos. They haven't lived a day and already I almost lost them."

"I would imagine many feel the way you do, but it is still a wonderful thing to have. Or so I have been told."

"What am I going to do, Lytos? Twins do not exist in this world."

Lytos waved his friend's worries away and laced his fingers behind his head. "Nonsense.

Twins have always existed. You let your mind get too worried about myths and prophecies."

"The Eternals cursed us with the inability to produce multiples, in fear that we would destroy this world. So, what changed?"

"Time, my friend. Time has changed everything. As it always has. Our people are dwindling—and fast. If this continues, our people will cease to exist. It is rare, and hardly spoken of, but many in my kingdom have conceived a second child."

"What? When did this start?"

Lytos straightened in his seat and shook his head. "This is not a curse, Caelum, and it has nothing to do with you or those two boys. Time changes all things."

"How long, Lytos?"

Lowering his arms to rest on his knees, Lytos met Caelum's eye. "Since about nine months ago."

Caelum paled as he looked back at his sleeping family.

"Caelum, this is not your fault. This is the Star's blessing. Do not let yourself be pulled into the depths of conspiracies. Even the strongest of us are still human, and humans are born to make mistakes."

Caelum rested his elbows on his knees and scrubbed his hands over his face. "The others are going to demand they go through the trials."

Lytos shrugged. "They can demand from afar. But the trials haven't been done in centuries."

"You don't think this will make them reconsider?"

"Let them try."

"They will come. The moment they hear, they will come."

Lytos met his friend's eye, a menacing light burning in their emerald depths. "Let them come."

"There will be war."

Lytos sighed. "Then we will fight."

Caelum furrowed his brow. "You would do that? For me and mine?"

Lytos arched a brow, a smirk playing at his lips. "What else do I have to do?"

Caelum barked out a harsh laugh and shook his head. "You should settle down, my friend. Start a family of your own."

"I can't do that. I'm too busy protecting yours." Chuckling, Lytos rose from his makeshift chair. Slapping a hand onto Caelum's shoulder, he asked the nagging question, "Have you named them?"

Caelum smiled for the first time in many hours. "We were always trapped between two. I suppose there is no reason to fight now."

"And?"

Caelum looked up with a mischievous glint in his eyes. "Hexius and Snip."

Lytos's eyes flared in surprise. "Really? Perhaps you *are* trying to curse them." Caelum flinched at the word and Lytos lifted a brow. "Too soon?"

"A mite," Caelum admitted.

Lytos shrugged and turned to leave. "I'll see to the nurse. Find out what I can. Maybe she is a part of the faction that seeks to bring down the Realm."

"Lytos," Caelum called.

"Hmm?"

Caelum glared at the chair. "You'd better fix that before you go. You know Evelyn doesn't appreciate your random additions to our home."

Lytos dropped his head back in boisterous laughter before waving his hand. Like an elegant dance between nature and creation, the tree's roots receded back into the floor, neatly piling the tiles back into place. Caelum grinned and turned his attention back to the trio that now held his heart. "Lytos?" he called once more.

His friend stopped and turned with a frown.

"Thank you."

Lytos looked over at Evelyn and the sleeping children with a sad smile. "Family is all we have in this world. It should be protected with every breath we take. A war has begun, Caelum. One that started long before those two were even a thought in your mind. This will inflame the situation, but remember, they are the greatest gift that the Stars could have given you."

"Thank you. Let me know what you get from the nurse."

Lytos's eyes darkened, and a menacing smile contorted his face. "Of course."

Caelum glared. "Do not overdo it. We need her for information. Keep your … fun to a minimum."

Lytos rolled his eyes and closed the door behind him. Caelum inhaled a deep, weighted breath and lost himself in the sight of his new family.

CHAPTER FIVE

The room was dark and cold. The definition of a dungeon, and yet, under the soft glow of the orbs, it looked mesmerizing, like constellations trapped within arm's reach. Beautiful. If you ignored the woman currently struggling against her bonds in the center.

Lytos took his time admiring the room. His eyes roamed over the ancient runes and forgotten symbols that hung in the air and fell like falling stars into its center. Each incandescent line held its own nefarious purpose. He rolled his shoulders and nodded to the two men that had been posted guard. Wordlessly, they filed out, and a smile lifted his lips as the soft click of the closing door resonated in the room. Taking another step, he found himself inside the circle, his eyes locked on the woman. She glared at him.

"Do you know what this room is?" he asked.

The woman's glare darkened.

Lytos tapped his finger against a column of falling symbols. "Each line is special. Though time has erased the full knowledge of what they say, their meaning is still known. Or, at least, *most* of them. Even after generations of tireless research, some remain lost in time. For example, this line keeps your screams from leaving this circle. I can step out any time and not hear a word." Lytos wandered around the circle and tapped a string of red runes. "This brings excruciating pain to anyone who lies."

The woman shifted in her chair, and Lytos smirked. He'd rattled her. "What do you want from me?" she asked.

Ignoring her question, Lytos continued around the circle, tapping the occasional column before continuing. "It's strange, but I find this room captivating. The history it holds. Did you know this castle was built around it? Sometimes, I come down here and wonder what terrible thing warranted the construction of such a room."

The woman snorted. "I think that is obvious."

Lytos paused. "Is it? What do you think its purpose is?"

"Torture."

Lytos nodded. "In part, yes," he conceded.

"You'll get nothing from me."

Lytos clasped his hands behind his back and rocked back on his heels. "We'll see."

Caelum jerked upright in his chair as a knock sounded on the door. Swiping a hand over his face, he rose and kissed each of his new family members on the forehead before opening the door a crack. Caelum frowned. "Radnar? What are you doing here? I didn't know Lytos let you leave his kingdom."

Radnar chuckled and scratched at his newly sprouting beard. "Sometimes. When he has a need for my *particular* skills. Lytos would like to have a word."

"Let's not keep him waiting, then." Caelum glanced over his shoulder before slipping through the door and shutting it softly behind him. "How are things?"

Radnar eyed the king out of the corner of his eye. "Slow."

Caelum smirked. "Not much of a talker, are you?"

Radnar shrugged as they turned down the long corridor.

"I have heard great things about you from Lytos. He claims you are his right hand. I found it surprising, considering how close he and Marcus have always been."

Radnar snorted.

Caelum dipped his head to hide his smile. "Agreed."

Radnar smirked and rapped twice on the plain wooden door. Caelum frowned at the man's twisted expression. "What is it?"

Radnar opened his mouth to speak when the door opened. Lytos beamed at them. "About time."

Caelum rolled his eyes and followed him inside. His eyes flared when he spotted the nurse. White fiery rage coursed through his veins at her nearly pristine appearance. His eyes narrowed as soundless tears trickled down her cheeks. "I thought you were getting information from her," he seethed.

Lytos chuckled and stepped into the circle. "There is more than one way to extract information. You like the more barbaric methods while I favor the mind."

"People will say anything to make physical pain end. But when you dig into the mind, it becomes all-consuming—unimaginable. Extorting the truth becomes easier," Radnar explained.

Caelum lifted a brow and glanced between the two. "This was you?" he asked Radnar.

Radnar clenched his jaw and turned his attention to the weeping woman.

"He has a rare ability. Doesn't like to use it often but will when it is necessary," Lytos whispered.

Caelum nodded. "What have you learned?"

"Straight to it then." Lytos pouted and tapped the woman's head, making her flinch and her lip tremble. "Alright, tell him what you told me."

The woman lifted her sweat-soaked face to meet Caelum's eyes. "My name is Lita. I am a descendent of Abraxas of the Original Kings. I was sent into this kingdom because of the books they left behind."

"What books?" Caelum asked.

Lita smirked. "You have all become so consumed by what you think this Realm is that you have been blinded to what is coming. The birth of your sons is only the beginning."

Caelum clenched his fists. "You tried to take them. Why? Who are you working with?"

Lita refused to answer, smirking.

"Radnar," Lytos sighed.

Lita's eyes flared with raw fear as Radnar moved closer. "They are the beginning of the end!" she shouted. "The Eternals thought that if they put an end to twins, they could stop what was to come. Except, Themis didn't agree and when your children were born, I knew it was starting."

"What was starting?"

"The beginning of the end. They are just the first piece in the prophecy: *'and the birth of two will breathe life into the vessels of Darkness and Light.'* Don't you see? We can stop it all if only you—"

"Where were you going to take them?"

"To Abraxas's crypt."

"Why?"

"Because only he can … cleanse them."

Caelum quivered. "You were going to leaving my newborn children as a sacrifice?"

"Caelum," Lytos warned. Caelum fisted his hands and clenched his eyes shut. Deep breaths puffed past his lips as he reined himself in. "Where are these books?" Lytos asked.

Lita cried out as she struggled against the charms. Her chest heaved as she struggled for breath until her body sagged in defeat. "In the tomb," she whimpered.

Lytos nodded to Radnar and, turning, pulled Caelum from the room with him.

"What is he going to do?" Caelum asked.

Lytos blew out a heavy breath. "You don't want to know."

"We need to get those books."

"And we will. *I* will."

"I'm coming with you."

Lytos shook his head. "You need to get back to your family. Spend time with them before Hadeon and his minions catch wind."

Caelum hesitated before his bedroom door. "Let me know when you have them."

Lytos nodded. "Of course. Now go. I'll buy you as much time as I can."

Caelum stood in silence as his friend disappeared. Running a hand through his hair, he dropped his head against the door. "Stars, what am I going to do?"

Chapter Six

For six days, Caelum basked in the resplendent glow of his new life as a father. Then, the first message arrived.

He paced the nursery, lightly bouncing Hex in his arms as he sang an old war tune, when the messenger burst in and slammed the door behind him. Caelum's eyes turned black as night as he placed Hex back into the cradle beside his brother. A tainted glow emanated from his skin—a warning.

Panting and covered in sweat, the messenger swayed in the doorway. Caelum narrowed his eyes. "What?" he snapped.

The man opened his mouth to speak as he struggled to catch his breath. "The-the kings … they are here. They are demanding to speak to you. I-I came as … as fast as I could, but I couldn't get to the portals before they—"

"Who sent you?"

"King Lytos."

Caelum's breakfast rolled in his stomach, but he didn't let his nerves show. He lifted a brow. "Where is he?"

The man shook his head. "He said he would be here as soon as he could. He is holding them off but—"

The door burst open. "Not well enough," one of the intruders chuckled.

Caelum clenched his jaw as three men strode into the nursery with malevolent smiles.

"Hello, Caelum. We heard your wife gave birth and came to congratulate you."

Caelum schooled his face into a bored expression as he took stock of the men standing in front of him. Hadeon, the most powerful Death Walker in centuries, led the pack. Dressed in his typical white attire, he looked like a phantom, not unlike those he reaped. He had stark white hair and silver eyes. His body was long, lanky, and when he moved, his robes billowed unnaturally, making him look like a ghost.

Next came Casimir with his light blonde hair and pale blue eyes. He was notorious for using his seer abilities to hold people hostage to his whims. Casimir sneered at Caelum, his pointed nose flaring in disgust. "We have been hearing whispers, Caelum. You are keeping a secret."

Caelum blinked innocently. "Whatever do you mean?"

The third intruder, Dorrin, stepped forward, his flaming red hair drifting over his muddy eyes. "You're glowing, Caelum. You may be able to lie, but your soul cannot."

Caelum's lip curled. "We have an agreement in place, Dorrin. We do not use our abilities on one another. Soul searching may be a useful tool, but don't forget that I am not one of your citizens. If you use your ability on me, I will do the same. How does the northernmost pole sound to you? I hear Jak has been in an awful mood lately."

Dorrin took another daring step forward, his intent apparent in the curling of his hands and the heat that rolled off his body in waves.

Suddenly, a chill cleansed the room, dousing Dorrin and bringing white puffs of vapor from everyone's lips.

"That's enough." Nalik's voice was icy as he strode into the room, the ground beneath his feet glossy with ice. His prismatic hair gleamed like sunbeams bouncing off freshly fallen snow. His eyes shone like the ocean. Irritated, he stalked to Caelum's side. Lytos swaggered in after him, light following him like a summer's sun.

While relief flooded his body at Nalik's and Lytos's arrival, Caelum was careful to keep his face inscrutable.

Hadeon broke the silence with a sickly sweet greeting. "How nice of you two to join us! We were afraid you might have gotten … *tied up* with something else."

Lytos snorted and crossed his arms over his chest. "Yes, I'm sure you did."

"Lytos," Nalik warned.

Lytos stroked his chin, unable to hide his amusement. "I heard there was some ruckus. Apparently, your men had some issues with one of the portals. Terrible thing when they go airy like that. Temperamental things, really. Especially when one enters with malicious intent."

Dorrin and Casimir gritted their teeth, their eyes darkening as their anger reached a boiling point. Hadeon slapped a hand on each of their chests, keeping them in check. He grinned. "I think we have gotten off on the wrong foot. After all, we cannot be held liable for what people do on their own time."

"You sent them after us and you know it," Lytos growled.

Hadeon leaned forward. "Prove it," he said with a smirk.

Lytos shook, his fury bubbling. "Oh, I will, Hadeon. I always get my answers. *Always.*"

"Are you going to sick your dog on us, Lytos?"

"That's enough," Nalik sighed. "While these games were fun as children, we are adults now. You were not invited to this kingdom and are in breach of the Seven Kings' Bond. State your business and be gone."

The infants' shrill cries filled the room as the temperature plummeted. Caelum cursed under his breath and turned to the crib. "Control yourself, Nalik," he snapped, rubbing his hands over both sons and cooing softly. "Hush now. It is only your Uncle Nalik showing off."

"Ah, yes. Right on cue," Hadeon said as he stepped forward.

Lytos stepped into his path. "Stay right there," he warned, his body glowing with a vibrant white light.

Hadeon pursed his lips in displeasure. "You would refuse to let an uncle meet his nephew? Or should I say *nephews?*"

"They are of no relation to you." While Caelum's words were harsh, his tone was soft as he looked upon the infants. The twins grew silent, only their lips trembling as their arms flailed around them. Caelum smiled as he carefully guided their searching hands to one another.

"There you are, all better." He chuckled as the pair gripped each other tightly and their eyes began to drift shut. Caelum adjusted the blanket to cover them, giving himself one last moment of peace before rejoining Lytos and Nalik.

"You know why we are here," Hadeon said.

Caelum shrugged. "To congratulate me?"

"We, three of the Seven Kings, demand the trials. If you refuse, we are prepared to sever the bond—sending us all into the depths of hell."

Lytos chuckled and crossed his arms over his chest. "You would, would you? Then do it."

For a moment, Hadeon's facade fell, his eyes widening in disbelief. Then his mask slammed back into place. "If we sever the bond, we all die. Then who will be here to protect your progeny?"

"I will."

All eyes turned to the newcomer, but it was Caelum's heart that squeezed. "Evelyn."

CHAPTER SEVEN

Evelyn hummed as she worked her hands over the blooming garden. She beamed as the wilted flowers lifted their heads to brush their petals against her skin.

"My lady!"

Evelyn jerked, turning to the panicked maid with wide eyes. "Lucy? What is it? What's wrong?"

"The Seven Kings! They have all come!"

The blood drained from her face so swiftly she had to steady herself on the ground. "Here?" she whispered. "Where?"

"The nursery, my lady."

Evelyn's mind raced. "He knew," she whispered. "He warned me."

The maid frowned. "Warned you? Who?"

Evelyn shook her head and scrambled to her feet. "We have to hurry!" she called, racing across the lush green grass. The world blurred around her as she swiped the tears from her eyes.

Evelyn smiled down at the bundle in her arms and carefully settled into one of the large armchairs. She had long since grown tired of swaying and pacing the large room and welcomed the reprieve as she curled her legs beneath her.

"Evelyn?"

"Shh," she whispered. "Snip is finally asleep."

Caelum smiled at his wife and settled into the armchair across from her. "So is Hex," he whispered back, leaning forward to show the dozing babe in his arms.

Evelyn smiled at the sight, her eyes lingering as she searched Hex's tiny face before turning her attention back to the one she held in her arms. Mesmerized, the couple sat in silence, losing themselves in the miracles they cradled in their arms. Caelum's eyes bounced from one child to the other and back again. His stomach twisted at the happiness on his wife's face. He loathed the world and the situation they found themselves in. "Evelyn?"

"Hmm?" Evelyn traced a finger down one of Snip's plump cheeks and over his Cupid's bow. His tiny lips twitched.

Caelum flinched at her smile, knowing he was about to shatter it completely. "Evelyn, we need to talk."

She looked up with panic and worry swirling in her grey eyes. "What is it?"

Caelum swallowed, the knot in his throat bobbing. "You know I am going to do everything in my power to protect our family."

Evelyn tightened her hold on Snip. "You're scaring me, Caelum."

Caelum's tongue swiped over his bottom lip. "I promise that is never my intention, but I want—need—you to be prepared for anything that may come our way."

"I don't understand. What's going to happen?" "You know twins are not … common in our world."

Evelyn sucked in a harsh breath. "Caelum—"

"There are some that will say they are unnatural. That they are an omen for what is to come."

Tears filled Evelyn's eyes, trailing her cheeks as she shook her head. "No, please…"

Caelum flinched at her plea. "Hadeon, Dorrin, and Casimir will demand the trials and—"

"NO!"

"Evelyn."

"NO! No, I won't allow it. They are children. Our children. They are innocent and good, and I will not let those monsters treat them like they are a science experiment."

Caelum stiffened at the words left unspoken. "And you think I will?"

Evelyn's eyes flashed with pain. "I think you will be left without a choice."

Fire burned in his eyes. "I would never let anyone, no matter who they are, hurt my family."

"But—"

Caelum frowned. "But?"

A sad smile tilted her lips. "Your words come with restrictions, Caelum. It is the world we live in. They are going to come for our children. I knew it from the moment the doctor spoke of another. We will be left helpless, and they will be defenseless."

Caelum leaned forward, careful of the bundle in his arms, and made a solemn vow: "I will protect them, Evelyn. Even if it means my life. I will not let harm come to them."

Evelyn shook her head, freeing a single tear from where it clung to her eyelashes. "You should not make promises you cannot keep."

Evelyn slowed as she drew closer to the nursery and, checking her surroundings, stopped in front of a towering portrait of a man with d bloodied grey wings battling an enormous wolf. She lifted a hand and brushed her fingertips across the great beast's side. After a few seconds, the picture began to shimmer, and Evelyn stepped through. Muffled voices filled the room, urging her forward. Careful not to make a sound, she scurried to hide behind a nearby pillar.

Hadeon wore a victor's smile as he spoke. "If you refuse, we are prepared to sever the bond and send us all into the depths of hell."

Lytos chuckled and crossed his arms over his chest. "You would, would you? Then do it."

For a moment, Hadeon's façade fell, his eyes widening in disbelief before his mask slammed back into place. "If we sever the bond, we all die. Then who will be here to protect your progeny?"

"I will," Evelyn snapped, stepping from the shadows.

"Evelyn! What are you doing here?" Caelum asked.

Evelyn arched a defiant brow. "You did not honestly believe I would let you take my children around these heathens without me, did you?"

Lytos clutched his chest. "You wound me, Evelyn."

"If only I had the power." Evelyn smiled. With daggers in her eyes, she focused on the menacing trio. Two stared at her newborns with excitement and fascination in their eyes while the third leered in her direction. "You will not submit my children to your barbaric acts."

Hadeon dropped his head to the side with an amused smile. "You have spoken as if you have a say."

A saccharine smile graced Evelyn's features as she met Hadeon's stare. "And you speak as if you have no will to live."

Hadeon's grin stretched unnaturally. "Are you threatening one of the Seven, Evelyn? How very daring of you."

"Only promises pass my lips, Hadeon. How is Paisley these days?"

Lytos barked out a laugh, quickly covering it with a cough. "I think I'm getting a cold," he lied.

Dorrin and Casimir glared at Lytos. Hadeon's smile fell, replaced by a deadly gleam in his eyes. "I would watch your tongue."

Evelyn stepped toward him, her chin held high. "Careful, Hadeon, your evil is showing."

"Evelyn," Caelum warned.

Evelyn whirled to face her husband. "You will not subject my children to these wicked tests. They were not created from evil, nor were they sent as an omen of terrible things to come. They are a blessing from the Stars."

Hadeon pursed his lips. "Would you care to prove your words?"

Caelum's eyes flared. "No."

"Yes," Evelyn vowed.

CHAPTER EIGHT

"Before we start with Evelyn, does everyone know the rules of the trials?" Hadeon asked.

Nalik shook his head. "We both know how this goes, Hadeon. I will write the rules on a binding scroll that will then be sealed with a blood bond."

"Whatever happened to 'my word is my bond'?" Hadeon said with a pout.

"You destroyed the value of your word the moment you began your games," Nalik muttered. Crossing the room, he dropped into Caelum's chair and withdrew a black scroll and silver feather from the bottom drawer of the king's desk. "Come on," he urged. "We haven't got all day, and I would like to get this over with."

One by one, they moved to stand before the desk, each holding out a hand.

"Lytos," Nalik called.

Lytos hesitated. "We shouldn't be entertaining their madness."

Nalik glanced at Caelum. "We don't have a choice. Three Kings have made a demand, and the law says—"

"The law says that a *majority* rule must be upheld. Three is not a majority."

Nalik's pupils lightened in color until they threatened to be swallowed by his sclera. "Do you really want to bring Orion into this? He is a child himself and barely able to speak. Do you believe he will make an adequate decision on the matter?"

Lytos clenched his jaw.

Caelum rested a hand on his friend's shoulder. "Lytos, he's right. We can't bring Orion into this. He isn't old enough to be pulled into politics."

"Then we should call upon Reaper."

A collective gasp filled the room. "You can't be serious. Do you even know what will happen if something like that is done? They were sealed away for a reason," Hadeon snapped.

Lytos smiled. "You would lose your case. The Old Ones do not believe in experimentation or subjecting children to the trials."

Evelyn's eyes brightened as a memory burst free in her mind. "Not all of them were sealed away."

The group turned toward her. "What?" Caelum asked.

Excitement lifted her lips. "Not all of them are sealed away. There is one who still walks these lands."

Hadeon rolled his eyes. "That is a myth, a legend. No one has seen Themis."

Evelyn lifted her chin and smirked. "I have."

"Evelyn!" Caelum snapped. Evelyn frowned and turned to look at her husband. "That's enough," he said, his voice softer now.

Hadeon stepped forward with a predator's grin. "No, please. Evelyn, tell us more."

"That's enough, Hadeon. Spell out the rules and let us get this over with. My sons will be awake from their nap soon, and I do not wish to tarnish them with the sight of you."

Hadeon let Caelum change the subject but kept his smile and his eyes on Evelyn. His grin did not falter.

Nalik nodded once more to Lytos, who grumbled under his breath but withdrew a golden dagger from his side; with a lightning-fast swipe, he sliced each king's finger. Dorrin jerked back as red began to weep from his mangled fingertip.

"Rather deep, don't you think?" he seethed.

Lytos kept his eyes on Nalik's. "Oops."

Nalik dipped his head to hide his own smile and turned the quill toward the bleeding group. "Hurry, before you ruin Caelum's rickety desk."

One by one, they lifted their punctured fingers and let seven drops fall upon the gleaming silver feather until it was stained. The droplets plopped against the delicate barbs, making them bounce under the added weight. The kings stepped back, leaving Nalik to hold the tarnished quill. Slowly the drops shifted, collecting into one another, before sliding to tainting the shinning nib.

A serious expression took over Nalik's face as he carefully unrolled the blackened scroll and began to write:

Initial question posed to the Seven Kings:

Does the birth of Hexius and Snip represent a bad omen from the Stars?

1. *All parties will be **honest** in using their abilities*

2. *No secrets will be kept from any of the Seven Kings*

3. *Any new information gained will be openly shared with **all** present parties*

4. *No malicious harm will come to **any** of the subjects undergoing the trials*

5. *All subjects will be treated with respect and **not** pushed beyond reasonable means*

6. *Anyone caught sharing the information gathered, or using it outside of the approval of all Seven Kings, will be sent into exile*

> 7.   *The trials will end when either a) the*
> *initial question has been answered or*
> *b) serious emotional/physical trauma*
> *occurs as determined by the parents*

Nalik leaned back and read over his work. After the third read-through, he nodded his head and turned the paper toward the other five for their appraisal. "Once you have finished reading, press your fingers to the bottom of the page."

Evelyn peered over Caelum's shoulder. "I don't understand. I thought I was going to be tested, not the twins."

Nalik propped his elbows on the desk and steepled his fingers. "You're right. You will be. This is just a precaution, and I would rather it be in place now, before tempers are … high." His eyes bounced from Caelum to Lytos.

Evelyn swallowed. "Right, of course."

Hadeon read over the document with a scowl, jabbing his finger upon rule seven. "This is not part of the original trials."

"True," Nalik said. "Except, the trials have never been done on a child before. Seeing as I am the eldest and strongest of us all, I make the rules. I would take what I have been given, Hadeon. Otherwise, I just might seek the Reaper."

Hadeon held his gaze but placed his fingerprint at the bottom. Dorrin and Casimir followed quickly behind. Lytos and Caelum exchanged an expressionless glance before reading. Caelum sucked in a breath. "Who determines an answer to that question? What I find to be an omen differs from yours—or Hadeon's."

Nalik considered this before swiping the paper back and changing the question to:

Is the birth of Hexius and Snip a sign from the Stars that the Realm will fall?

Hadeon glanced over the document and slammed his teeth together.

Nalik smirked as he looked at the man. "Is there a problem, Hadeon?"

Hadeon forced a smile. "Of course not, Nalik."

"Good, now you two, sign."

Lytos glared, but placed his thumb against the bottom of the scroll. Caelum inhaled deeply before slowly releasing it and placing his thumbprint beside Lytos's.

Nalik stood, placing his thumbprint as the final seal. "It's time," he said, meeting Evelyn's eyes.

CHAPTER NINE

Curiosity killed the wandering cat. Or something like that. Evelyn's mind was a mess as she followed the group through the castle and down a hidden set of stairs. Her body vibrated with nerves and excitement at exploring the hidden passage. Over the years, she had discovered more of its layout than Caelum even knew of. Evelyn shook herself. This wasn't a time for wandering the castle. Her newborns were at stake.

The narrow stairway opened to a large room that instantly came to life upon their arrival. Hundreds of miniature glowing orbs littered the high ceiling, reminding her of the moonless night sky. "It's beautiful," she whispered.

Caelum squeezed her hand. "You're right. Another time, maybe we will come back and wipe this place of its terrible past."

"What terrible past?"

"Alright, let's get started!" Hadeon clapped his hands together in excitement, interrupting Caelum's answer. Evelyn's mouth went dry as she found Hadeon motioning her toward a large stone block that looked to be stained with a questionable liquid. Ancient symbols littered the sides in swirling, staggered patterns.

"Absolutely not. I am not going to that sacrificial stone!"

Caelum squeezed her hand once more. "The chair will suffice, Hadeon."

Hadeon pouted but nodded to Casimir, who withdrew the rickety-looking chair from the equally rickety-looking table. "Fine."

"Lytos will do the pricking with his dagger. Not you and yours," Caelum snapped when Dorrin lifted a dirtied blade from the table.

Hadeon rolled his eyes. "Anything else?"

"You will not test further than the length of her pregnancy," Nalik added.

Hadeon tipped his head in curiosity. "Is there something you are afraid for us to know?" "Men like you do not wield knowledge with grace," Nalik murmured sagely.

Hadeon rolled his eyes. "Come, dear Evelyn, take a seat in my chair."

Evelyn moved before she could convince herself to run. She settled in the chair, offering to the dagger-wielding king. "Now, Lytos," she pleaded, afraid she would lose her nerve.

Lytos's hand wrapped around her wrist. "Sorry, Evie."

Evelyn hissed as the blade split her palm.

"Hurry or I'll heal it myself," Nalik snapped.

Dorrin stepped forward with a terrifying gleam in his eyes and plunged his finger into her wound. Evelyn cried out, and Caelum, Nalik, and Lytos rushed forward.

"That isn't necessary!" Caelum growled.

Hadeon shrugged. "You never said *how* he had to read her. He prefers the up-close approach."

Dorrin pulled his finger back, and with it came a thick, twisted green and white strand. "She has been tampered with. Her pregnancy was unnatural."

Evelyn jerked her hand from his grasp and shook her head. "That isn't true! Caelum—"

Dorrin lifted the strand between thumb and forefinger. "This says otherwise."

"We used no magical interference to conceive," objected Caelum.

"Bragging now?" Lytos chuckled. A whoosh of air left his lungs as Nalik smacked a hand against his chest.

"Was her pregnancy unnatural—or the delivery?" Nalik asked.

Dorrin hesitated.

"You cannot lie, Dorrin," Nalik reminded him. Lytos smiled and tapped a shimmering rune strand.

Dorrin's jaw jumped in frustration. "I cannot confidently say."

"What *can* you say? Confidently."

Dorrin glanced to Hadeon, who watched curiously. "Evelyn, did you seek help while pregnant?"

Evelyn swallowed through growing panic. "Yes," she admitted. "Caelum, I promise, she did nothing to harm—"

"Who?"

"Themis," she replied.

Hadeon gasped. "She lies! She—"

"What are you saying?" Nalik interrupted.

"The person you saw may have corrupted the fetus, tearing it in two and going against nature. The trials must be done," Dorrin explained. Hadeon chuckled.

Caelum's stomach twisted as Lita's words slipped through his mind like poison. Evelyn broke. Her strength drained away as she fell to her knees and hugged her stomach. *It's all my fault. I should have just let it take me...*

"As you can see, I have already been proven correct," Hadeon boasted. "Now, give me your spawn so that I may understand their existence."

Evelyn groaned as guilt continued its unrelenting assault.

"Hadeon," Nalik called.

Hadeon turned with an overly schooled, bored expression. "What is it now, Nalik?"

Nalik leaned against the wall, his legs crossed at the ankles as he coolly examined his fingernails. "I do believe you read the contract, correct?"

Hadeon rolled his eyes. "Yes, yes. I know your rules, Nalik. Don't worry, I have no intention of breaking any of them."

Nalik pushed from the wall with a smile. "Oh, but you already have."

"How dare you!" Hadeon seethed, stomping forward until he was forced to look up into Nalik's eyes. "I signed your contract, followed your rules with Evelyn, and now you dare say that I have breeched the contract? Are you searching for a way to send me into exile?" His hot breath ruffled Nalik's hair.

Nalik smirked and withdrew the black scroll from his pocket. "Yes, always. However, this time it will be your doing."

Hadeon scowled as he snatched the scroll from Nalik's hand and turned his back. He chuckled. "There is nothing here that proves I have broken the agreement."

Nalik leaned forward, peeking over Hadeon's shoulder. "Keep unrolling."

Curious, Hadeon unfurled more of the scroll and began to quake with rage. Hadeon dropped the scroll and whirled to face Nalik's knowing grin. "You tricked me!" Hadeon cried. "You tricked us all! This will not stand!"

The remaining kings rushed forward, fighting for the spellbound script. Caelum was first. With trembling hands, he unfurled the scroll and released a weighted breath.

***The trials will begin six months from the moment of this contract's enactment.*

They will be held once a year for four hours until either a) the initial question has been answered or b) serious emotional/physical trauma is exhibited as deemed by the parents.

*This contract is binding and cannot be changed once all six parties have signed***

You should have read closer, Hadeon.

Caelum read the last passage over and over until Lytos pried the black parchment from his fingers and clapped a hand upon his back. "It is not what we wanted, but it is better than what we thought," Lytos whispered.

Caelum slipped away from the group and pulled his wife to her feet. Evelyn's body shook with the force of her silent sobs. "Evelyn," he croaked.

Evelyn lifted red-rimmed eyes to her husband. "Caelum? What is it?"

"Nalik. He bought us time. He saved our sons."

Evelyn swiped her hands across her eyes, shaking her head. "What? How?"

Caelum's cheeks puffed as he released an incredulous breath. "I-I don't... I don't know, Evie. But he did."

"He used trickery!" Hadeon raged. "He hid the clause at the end of the curled page! The contract is void!"

Nalik's laid-back demeanor changed in an instant. His smile vanished and his body tensed. The temperature plummeted to a bitter chill. "I gave you the contract, Hadeon. I cannot be held responsible for your inattentiveness. To declare this contract void is to spit upon my honor and worth within the Seven Kings. Do you have enough of a hold to displace me?"

Hadeon clenched his jaw to stifle the chattering of his teeth and turned his attention to Caelum. "Soak it up all you want now. But I'll be back, and the trials will begin."

"Alright, I think it is time for you three to leave before we all end up with frostbite," Lytos snickered.

Hadeon cast one last glare around the room before leaving in a flurry of white robes.

Evelyn sprinted across the room and threw her arms around Nalik's waist. "Thank you, thank you, thank you."

Nalik stiffened under the sudden show of emotion. He gently patted her back with one hand while the other remained stiff at his side. "Yes. You're welcome. I only wish I could have done more."

Evelyn shook her head against his chest. "No, you did more than enough."

"Evelyn, my love, you are making him uncomfortable." Caelum chuckled.

Evelyn pulled back with a smile. "I will forever be in your debt."

"Then I wish to cash in."

"Evelyn," Caelum cautioned. Though Nalik was a friend, and a close one at that, making a promise to someone with his power was dangerous.

Ignoring her husband, Evelyn promised, "Anything."

"Where did you meet Themis?"

CHAPTER TEN

Six months later

Evelyn's stomach twisted, rising and falling like the acid in her throat. She hadn't slept in two days. Her mind revolted at the powerless state she found herself in. She was a mother. She was supposed to protect her children no matter what, but instead, she was forced to let the most corrupt men in the Realms experiment on them.

Tears swam in her eyes as she stared down at Hex and Snip. Their dark hair was mussed from sleep. Their perfect pink lips were parted as they softly snored. Six months of bliss had passed too swiftly for her liking. They had grown like weeds, smiled often, and radiated joy and innocence.

A tear slipped down her cheek as she swallowed a sob. She traced her icy finger over their cheeks, making Hex's nose scrunch and lip tremble. As if sensing his brother's distress, Snip rolled onto his side and blindly searched for his brother's hand. Once he found it, he wrapped his small fingers around his brother's and, in unison, their bodies sagged into the mattress, slipping back into their peaceful slumber.

"Evelyn?" Caelum whispered, so as to not wake them. "What are you doing in here? Are they alright?"

Evelyn took a shaky breath and swiped the tears from her cheeks. "They are fine. I just like to watch them sleep."

Caelum's heart squeezed at the distress that oozed from her pores. He stepped into the room and let the door shut soundlessly behind him as he made his way to her side. A smile crested his lips as he looked down at the perfect pair they had made. "It's late and tomorrow is going to be a long day. Why don't you get some sleep, and I will stay with them?"

Evelyn shook her head and felt the burn of fresh tears prick her eyes. "No. I don't want to leave them."

Caelum squeezed the tops of her arms in reassurance and pressed a kiss to the side of her head. "Alright then. We will sleep here. I'll be right back."

The air rustled behind her as Caelum snapped his fingers and opened a portal. He slipped through the shimmering opening; here one moment and gone the next. Moments later, he reemerged, pushing the oversized armchair that typically sat in the corner of their bedroom.

At the scrape of wood on stone, Evelyn turned, her mouth dropping open. "What are you doing?"

Caelum looked up with a smile and spread his arms wide. "I know you love this chair and if we are going to be staying here tonight, we should at least be comfortable." His smile fell, lips twisting into a frown as he looked around. "You don't think the bed will fit in here, do you? Or we could just bring them into our room."

A giggle slipped through her lips, and Evelyn slapped her hand over her mouth, shaking her head. "No, Caelum. I do not believe our bed will fit in here. Though the thought of bringing them into our room is tempting."

Caelum smiled as his wife's laughter sprinkled the room like glitter. "I missed that sound," he whispered.

Evelyn lifted joyful eyes to her husband. "What do you mean?"

"Your laugh. It has been days since I have heard it."

Evelyn's smile turned sad as she looked back at her slumbering children. "I am afraid, Caelum."

Caelum settled himself into the large chair and opened his arms. "Come," he urged. Hesitating, Evelyn nibbled at the inside of her cheek. Caelum lifted a brow and teased, "Do you deny your king?"

Evelyn rolled her eyes at his words but slipped into his embrace. Caelum smiled as he pulled the blanket over them both. Evelyn sighed as his heat chased away the chill she hadn't realized had settled into her bones.

"Would you tell me a story?" he asked.

"What kind of story?" Evelyn asked through a yawn.

"How did you meet Themis? And why didn't you tell me?"

Evelyn sighed. "I didn't want you to worry. You have so much on your shoulders, I didn't want to add to it."

"You're my wife, the mother of my children. There is nothing you can say or do that I wouldn't want to know about."

"I'm sorry, Caelum. I never expected this to happen."

"Will you tell me how it did? How I never noticed?"

Evelyn nodded and relaxed into his arms. "Alright. But it is a boring story," she warned.

Caelum kissed the side of her head. "Nothing about you is boring, my love."

CHAPTER ELEVEN

One Year Ago

Evelyn hummed to herself as she moved through the garden, tapping her finger against the delicate petals of the wilting flowers. She smiled when they lifted their heads and stretched toward the sky.

"Evelyn!"

Evelyn's eyes twinkled excitedly at the voice. Turning on her heel, she opened her arms just in time to catch her friend in a tight hug. "Solastra! What are you doing here?"

Solastra pulled back with a mock frown. "That is a terrible way to greet your dearest friend, Evie."

Evelyn rolled her eyes and smiled. "Of course, it is wonderful to see you! How have you been?"

Solastra pushed her raven hair over her shoulder and looped an arm through her friend's. "Come, I have so much to tell you." She paused when she noticed Evelyn's slightly rounded stomach. "Evelyn! You're pregnant!"

Evelyn smiled and ran a hand over her slightly rounded stomach. "Yes, I am. I would have told you, but you aren't the easiest person to get a hold of."

Solastra's brow pinched. "Do you mind?" she asked, her hand hovering above Evelyn's stomach.

Evelyn shook her head, confused at her friend's reaction.

Solastra reached a trembling hand forward and closed her eyes when her palm rested upon Evelyn's stomach. Sweat broke out along the top of her lip and her mouth went dry. Clearing her throat, she opened her eyes and searched the garden. "Let's take a seat." Wrapping her hand around Evelyn's wrist, she pulled her to a nearby bench and sat down.

"Solastra? Is everything alright?"

Solastra looked off into the distance, her chest rising and falling with calculated breaths. "I have been traveling through the Seven Kingdoms, healing and helping those in need. Those that their kings have deemed unworthy of their healer's aid."

Evelyn frowned. "That is great, Solastra, but I don't understand why you look so worried."

"I met her, you know. I was hurt. Ambushed by some of the unseelie. My fault, really, for wandering in the dark forest with no charms or protections in place."

"Met who?"

Solastra continued as though Evelyn never spoke, too lost in her own memories. "I escaped. Jak and Nalik taught me a few protection charms that came in handy, but I was pretty beat up and passed out on the edge of the forest. Right before I blacked out, I saw the forest shimmer. I figured it was because I had lost so much

60

blood, but when I woke up, I was in a strange place and this elderly woman was standing by my side." Solastra smiled. "She saved me, and I think she can save your child."

Evelyn paled, her stomach clenching. "What do you mean, 'save my child'? Who is she?"

Solastra turned to Evelyn. "Her name is Themis and I need you to come with me before—"

Pain ripped through Evelyn's abdomen. Air rushed from her lungs and the world dimmed. Her vision swam as the pain came in sharp, ceaseless waves. As one crested, another began. Warmth seeped into her hands, chasing away the darkness that threatened her vision.

Oxygen filled her lungs and cleared her mind. Evelyn frown at the sight of Solastra kneeling in front of her, tightly gripping her hands. "Evelyn, I know this is scary, but you have to come with me. Right now."

"Caelum," she groaned. "I have to get Caelum."

Solastra shook her head. "There isn't time. You have to come right now."

"I remember very little of what happened next. One minute I was in the garden, hunched over in pain, and the next I was in a tree with Solastra and a strange woman was leaning over me. The air smelled sweet but left a bitter taste on my tongue, and I felt my body relaxing—the pain dissipated with every subsequent breath. Words I didn't recognize filled my mind and sparks of light flashed behind my eyelids. I don't know how much time had passed. All I know is that, when I woke, the pain was gone and an energy I hadn't felt before filled my body. I later learned that the woman's name was Themis. She told me that the soul I was carrying was too much for its body and she fixed it. We returned to the garden just before nightfall, and no one seemed to notice I was ever gone."

Caelum struggled to comprehend the magnitude of it all. He ran through the story again and again.

"Are you angry?" she asked after several silent minutes passed.

Caelum pulled back and tapped a finger under her chin, lifting her eyes to his. "Never," he swore. "You saved them, Evelyn. None of this is your fault. It happened as the Stars demanded."

"I should have told you."

Caelum shrugged. "Yes, I wish you had come to me. But seeing what we have now…" He shook his head. "I wouldn't have it any other way."

A deliberate knock pulled their attention and stiffened their bodies. Caelum swallowed through the thickness in his throat and helped Evelyn to her feet. "Yes?" he called, his eyes locked on his wife.

The door opened on silent hinges, revealing Lytos bathed in a soft glow. "It's time."

Tears filled Evelyn's eyes. "I don't think I can do this."

Caelum forced a smile and rubbed his hands up and down her arms. "Everything is going to be alright."

Evelyn searched his eyes and found only strength. "How can you be so sure?"

"Because we won't let anything bad happen. Nothing you told me leads me to believe otherwise. The contract states no harm shall come to them. I know this isn't what we want, but it is what we have to do. Four hours, my love."

Resignation weighed heavily upon their shoulders. Caelum kissed her forehead and, together, they turned to the crib, each collecting a child. Evelyn kept her lips pressed to Snip's forehead as she, Caelum, and Lytos made their way through the castle.

A set of large, plain, black doors loomed ahead. It wasn't the sight of the doors that had Evelyn's heart racing, but the intricate carvings of angels casting demons into pits while their gods looked on, never lifting a finger to help.

Hadeon, Dorrin, and Casimir waited at the threshold with eager looks etched into their twisted faces. Evelyn's steps faltered as she tightened her grip on Snip. Caelum adjusted Hex on his hip and placed a hand on her lower back, urging her forward.

"If we break the contract, the rules apply to us as well," he whispered.

Evelyn took a deep breath and lifted her chin. *Show no weakness,* she reminded herself. Two women she didn't recognize appeared in the doorway with sad smiles and outstretched arms. Caelum frowned.

"They are from my castle," Lytos explained. "They will keep us informed of any misdeeds."

While his words were spoken to Caelum and Evelyn, there was a clear warning laced throughout. "Let the trials begin." Hadeon smiled.

Chapter Twelve

Two Years Later

With every passing year he was forced to submit his children to the trials, Caelum felt a piece of his mind plunge into madness. While the twins appeared to come out of the last three trials, seemingly unharmed, they always came back with a dimness in their eyes and their skin pale and clammy. When they would question the two attendants that Lytos sent in, they would only shrug and promise that everything went as it was supposed to.

Caelum didn't trust it and, in an effort to ease his friend's suffering, Lytos began to choose the watchers on a raffle basis.

"Four hours, Hadeon. Your time has begun," Caelum snapped.

Hadeon smirked and saluted him as the doors clicked shut. Evelyn sagged in the chair Caelum had brought, her slender shoulders shaking as she silently wept. Caelum knelt and took her hands in his. "Lytos has come with news. Would you like to come with me?"

Evelyn wiped her cheeks and shook her head. "I'll wait here."

Caelum flinched at the pain seeping from her pores. "If you need me, just call." Placing a kiss on her forehead, he strode down the hall to the room where Lytos and Nalik waited for him.

"We need more time! These translations are best guesses!" Nalik's booming voice slipped beneath the door.

Caelum dropped his head and shoved the door wide. "Would you mind keeping it down? I heard you halfway down the hall."

"Worried about spies, Caelum?" Lytos teased.

Caelum's eyes darkened. "We can trust no one. The walls wear more than one set of ears these days."

"Ray of sunshine today, aren't you?"

"Aren't I always? What have you found?" Caelum asked, looking over the cluttered table. Every available space was covered with old, tattered books, each opened to a different page, and loose slips of papers with elegantly scrawled notes.

Lytos fell into the chair behind him. "Not much, I'm afraid. These books…" He shook his head. "Half of them are written in a language no one knows. We think it was the original language of the Eternals."

Caelum frowned and picked up the one closest to him. It was a beautiful black leather-bound book with thin silver vines laced throughout the binding. His eyes washed over the strange metallic symbols that covered the cream-colored pages. His head began to throb within seconds. With a frown, he set it on the littered tabletop.

"It hurts, doesn't it?" Nalik asked.

Caelum looked up and found both Nalik and Lytos staring at him with interest. "What do you mean?"

"Staring at the symbols. It makes your head throb and eyes burn. As if you haven't blinked in hours, but it's only been a moment."

"Gets worse if you try to fight through it and read longer," Lytos said with a humorless chuckle.

"You both knew and didn't tell me?"

Nalik shrugged. "They affect everyone differently. It would be a lie if we said we weren't curious."

"It's always a pleasure being a part of your experiments, Nalik," Caelum snapped. "Now tell me, what have you found?"

"I would sit if I were you," Lytos mumbled, tossing him a thin stack of papers.

Frustration bubbled beneath Caelum's skin as he sat and scanned over the sheets. He shook his head. Disjointed lines of prophecy covered the pages, fractured but pieced together into best guesses. *The birth of two shall breathe life into the vessels of Darkness and Light. When life meets death, a child of azure will be born, and destruction will follow. As one of minds turns from right, Darkness will be unleashed.* "This is it? It's been two years and all you have is three pieces of paper?!"

Nalik sighed. "Translating ancient text isn't as easy as one would expect."

"There is nothing in here that can help us!"

"Caelum—" Lytos began.

"No! I can't keep sending my children through Hadeon's trials."

Nalik's face crumpled with sympathy. "I understand your plight, but the watchers say they are doing nothing to harm them. We may have to let this run its course."

"Do you understand? Do either of you? I am forced to stand by helplessly as a madman experiments on my children under the guise of keeping the Realm safe. My wife cries for weeks leading up to this day every year and is inconsolable for the four hours they are gone from her sight. How long must I let this continue?"

Blinding light filled the room as Lytos lurched to his feet, his hands slamming against the table. "How dare you!" he spit out, the papers rustling. "We are right here with you. We love those boys and treat them as our own. We abandoned our own futures to help you carve out theirs and you dare to sit there and act as though none of this affects us?"

The heated air cooled as Nalik stepped between the glaring pair. "That's enough. We cannot turn against one another now. Just because we don't have the answers we want now doesn't mean we won't in the future. I have people scouring these documents day in and day out. Men are searching the lands for any trace of where the Eternals have gone. We will get our answers, Caelum, but we must be patient."

Caelum scrubbed his hands over his face and dropped back against his chair. "I'm sorry, Lytos. I know this pains you two as well. It's just … hard to know you can't save your children. You will understand one day."

Lytos dropped into his chair with a snort. "I don't think so. After experiencing it all with you, I think I will be fine never having children."

"We'll see." Caelum grinned.

Nalik chuckled and lifted the largest and most unique looking tome in the collection. "Alright, before we go setting Lytos up, how about we focus on one problem at a time?"

Caelum frowned as he straightened to inspect the book. Red, orange, and yellow leaves were strung together to create both the cover and the pages inside. The pattern appeared to be random and erratic. "Where did you get that one?"

"From the tomb, with the rest of them. Why?" Lytos asked.

"The pattern. Doesn't it seem familiar to you?"

Nalik frowned and flipped through the pages. "No. Does it to you?"

"I think so … maybe?"

"I got it! The chamber!" Lytos declared. Leaping from his chair, he plucked the book from Nalik's hands and raced toward the door. "Come on!"

Caelum and Nalik spared a glance at each other before running after Lytos. Frightened shrieks filled the air, mingled with the slap of heavy steps as the three men raced down the halls. "Sorry!" Caelum called over his shoulder.

"Excuse us!" Nalik hollered, his hand motioning people to the side.

The glow surrounding Lytos's body brightened as the wooden, iron clad dungeon doors came into sight. A growl rumbled Caelum's chest as the memory of Lita's deceit flashed to the forefront of his brain.

Lytos barely skidded to a stop before throwing the doors wide and running inside. The chamber was empty and silent, except for the soft shimmer of the symbols under the orb's soft glow. "See?" Lytos smiled, pleased with himself.

Nalik and Caelum shook their heads, their hands resting on their hips as their chests rose with quick breath. "See what?" Nalik asked.

Lytos rolled his eyes and pointed to the patterned leaves, then to the columns. "Red, green, yellow. Red, orange, yellow. Orange, orange, yellow, green. The pages match the way the symbols fall!"

"But what does that mean?" Caelum asked.

Lytos shook his head but glowed with excitement. "I don't know, but I'm going to find out."

Chapter Thirteen

Four Years Later

Nalik swiped the books and papers from his desk, sending them crashing to the floor. Ice crawled up the windows and spread like spider webs from his feet. His chest heaved with frantic breath, the struggle to contain his anger a losing battle. He threw his head back and released a terrifying roar to the ceiling above, flooding the room with his icy power. Long, razor sharp icicles glittered dangerously from the crossbeams and chandelier. Snow fell in heavy sheets, covering the room in several inches of white powder.

Nalik dropped his chin to his chest and felt only marginally better. An upbeat knock sounded against his door and opened before he could allow or deny the unwanted intrusion.

His narrowed eyes burned with an icy fury. "Solastra, what are you doing here?" His tone was light, conflicting with both his defensive posture and the current state of his office.

Solastra arched a brow and stepped farther into the room. "Rough day, brother?"

Nalik's jaw clenched, a retort on the tip of his tongue when another stepped through the door. "Jak," he seethed.

Jak rolled his eyes and closed the door, leaning back against it. "Nalik." His sour tone rivaled his elder brother's as he crossed his arms. "I like what you've done with the place. Strange, given your ire when I do the same thing."

Solastra stomped her foot against the snow-covered floor, the sound muffled. "That's enough! I did not bring you here to bicker."

Jak arched a brow, his signature playful smirk revealing his vibrant white teeth. "Then why did you bring me here?"

"Yes, Solastra, why did you bring *him* here?"

Solastra clenched her jaw at the childish jab. "I brought him here to help you."

Nalik snorted and shook his head. "I don't need anyone's help. Especially his."

"So, you have found Themis, then? Saved Hex and Snip from Hadeon's nefarious experiments? Put a stop to the inevitable fall of the Realm?"

Jak's eyes widened as he shoved from the door. "What is she talking about?"

Nalik glared at his sister. "Nothing."

"It didn't sound like nothing. Who are Hex and Snip? Why do you need Themis and when is the Realm falling, *exactly*?"

Nalik tore his glare from his sister's knowing smirk and focused it on their brother. "You would know if you bothered to leave your self-appointed throne."

Angrily, Jak stalked forward with ice in his eyes. "You told me to leave, Nalik. You can't be angry at me for doing as you commanded."

"You left your family!" Nalik thundered.

"What family?!"

"ENOUGH!" Solastra screamed. The room shook and icicles fell from the ceiling, leaving Nalik and Jak to either jump away from one another or be speared. "You two are the most selfish people I have ever met. And I've met Reaper!"

The brothers frowned at each other before turning quizzical glances to their sister. "You've met Reaper?" Jak asked curiously.

At the same Nalik demanded, "When did you meet Reaper?"

Solastra waved the question away. "Have you found Themis, or do you need our help?"

Nalik's frown deepened. "You *both* know Themis?"

Jak shrugged. "Who doesn't?"

Solastra sank her teeth into her bottom lip to hold back her smile. Nalik threw his arms in the air. "I can't believe this. Both of my siblings know an Immortal and never thought to share it with their elder brother."

"You never asked," Jak snickered.

"Nalik, can you…" Solastra waved a hand around the room.

Nalik flicked his wrist and the snow and ice melted away into nothing, bringing the room's temperature back up. Jak pulled at his shirt, wafting the neck to cool himself down. "Great, now I'm sweating," he mumbled.

Solastra snapped her fingers and dug into her pocket. "That reminds me. Here you go, Jak. It took longer than I thought to find, but this should help."

Jak eyed the flat, rectangular, blue crystal with skepticism. "What is it?"

"Just take it. It'll help regulate your body temperature."

Jak took the pendant and lost himself inside the swirl of falling snow inside. "Where did you get it?"

"Not important. Nalik, are you ready?"

"Ready? For what?" Nalik asked.

"To get Themis. We haven't much time and Themis can be … stubborn."

Jak snorted and slipped the pendent over his head. A puff of white air left his lips. "Much better. Though I wouldn't say she's stubborn. More like … *immoveable* after she makes a decision."

Solastra nodded in agreement. "Exactly. Which means we need to go now."

"Why now?" asked Nalik.

"Evelyn told me you asked for more time—that this is the last trial the twins are going to go through. We need Themis to come forward if we don't want war."

"Then what are we waiting for?"

Jak and Solastra led him to a strange man with unique abilities in the darkest reaches of his kingdom. And while he was hesitant to deal with the man and his unusual portals, his siblings didn't seem to mind.

"Thanks again," Solastra waved at the wiry man and stepped through the portal with Jak on her heels. With a deep breath, Nalik forced one foot in front of the other until he was through and found himself deep in the black forest.

"What are we doing here?" he asked.

"Just wait," Jak answered.

Nalik bounced on his toes as time continued to tick by. "We don't have ti—" The words died on his tongue when the forest began to shimmer and fade before his eyes. Even in the Realm of magic, this was something he had never seen before. The dark, charred woods melted away, giving birth to towering, sky-piercing trees in every shade. Vibrant flowers littered the forest flower in shapes and colors he had never seen before. Scents—both rich and sour—filled his nose and lingered on his tongue.

Before Nalik could examine the new world unfolding around him, a petite, elderly woman with flowing silver hair and white eyes stepped out from behind a thick tree with a basket tucked tightly against her side.

"Solastra, is that you? And Jak too. What a treat!"

Solastra smiled and hugged the woman. "Hello Themis."

"Get over here and give me a hug, Jak," Themis ordered.

Red colored Jak's cheeks as he moved to do as the older woman instructed.

Themis peered around Jak's larger form. "Is that Nalik I see?"

Nalik cleared his throat and nodded. "Yes, ma'am."

Themis chuckled, an earthly sound. "None of that. You will make me feel older than I am." Nalik blushed and looked to his feet. "Now," she sighed, "what brings you to my neck of the woods?"

Solastra nibbled at her cheek. "We need you to come with us. We need your help."

Themis clucked her tongue and set the basket on a raised tree root. "What is it? Has something happened?"

"It's the twins."

Themis frowned. "Are they hurt?"

"They have been forced to undergo the trials," Nalik explained. "I did what I could to make it easier on the parents, but I am afraid Hadeon will not stop."

"Jak, would you work your magic on my sprites, please? And the winter blossoms, too. They have been neglected by you for too long," Themis chided.

"Themis," Solastra sighed. "I know you have your rules but—"

Themis lifted a hand. "I am sorry, Solastra, but I cannot interfere in the affairs of this Realm.

I have already done too much when I helped dear Evelyn."

"If you don't come with me, Hadeon is going to destroy their innocence. He says they are an abomination—that they are going to bring about the fall of the Realm. They wake with nightmares that rumble throughout the kingdom. Their souls are darkening, and we are powerless to stop it."

Themis narrowed her eyes. "The trials do not cause such things."

"I know. But we have no proof that what Hadeon is doing is the cause. He uses the fact of their unnatural creation as an excuse. But if you come with us, you can tell them. You can back Evelyn's claims. Please."

Themis stood in silent contemplation before placing her hands on the raised roots and moving her lips in a soundless chant. When she was done, she patted her hands against her pale dress and nodded. "Alright then, let us go. They have already left the chamber," she said, striding purposely toward a far tree.

Nalik frowned. "What?"

Themis slapped a hand against her hip. "Do you want to stop this or not?"

Nalik looked to his siblings who shrugged at him before disappearing into the tree after Themis.

CHAPTER FOURTEEN

Evelyn paced, her brow covered in sweat. Her hands twisted repeatedly at her waist. She glanced up at the fluttering butterflies that circled the large weeping, rainbow flower. The soft hum of their wings buzzed in her ears as they drifted around the dwindling bloom. Dew drops fell from the multi-colored petals of time, tracking the seconds as they ticked. Evelyn blew out a shaky breath. Her mouth was growing increasingly dry with each passing moment.

"They should be done already," she snapped as she continued to pace, nibbling at her fingernails while her stomach rolled and her heart slammed against its cage.

Caelum helplessly watched his wife. "They know the contract, Evelyn. They will be out any moment."

Lytos straightened from the wall he had been leaning against. "You have to calm down. The boys are going to be fine. The decision has been made."

Evelyn bit at her bottom lip. "This is the last time," she vowed. "They will never have to go back."

Caelum nodded. "That's right. This is the last time."

Evelyn repeated the words, mumbling them under her breath like a mantra to cool her burning soul. Six years had passed since Hadeon, Dorrin, and Casimir had begun the trials. Once a year, for four hours, they were forced from their children while the kings conducted unseen tests. At first, Hex and Snip had been fine. There were no wounds or ill effects to show that anything was amiss, and while both Evelyn and Caelum loathed the trials, they let them continue.

Then, last year, the nightmares had begun.

The first had brought Evelyn to her knees. The night had started like any other. Together, she and Caelum put the twins to bed, kissed their foreheads, and prayed for the Stars to watch over them. Then, in the depth of the night, the castle began to shake, and screams severed the peace. Caelum and Evelyn were ripped from their own slumber and raced down the hall to find both Hex and Snip sitting in their bed, gripping their heads as tormented screams shook their chests.

They didn't sleep for two nights after that. Caelum called a meeting with Lytos and Nalik, revealing what the boys had shared with them.

There will be no more trials, he'd said. At the news, Lytos lost his natural luster until his complexion rivaled the dead. Nalik's urgency to find Themis reached unprecedented levels.

"I need time," Nalik insisted.

Evelyn shook her head. "We can't. Not again."

"Please," he begged. "One last time. We need solid evidence they are breaking the contract."

"You said we could end the trials!"

Nalik nodded. "And we will. We just need one last time." His eyes moved to Caelum. "Please."

Caelum hesitated. His need to protect his children warred with the need to save his Realm. He turned to Lytos. "Have you deciphered anything from the book?"

Lytos shifted from foot to foot, his eyes dark with failure. "Nothing of value."

Caelum looked to his wife as tears filled her eyes. "This is the last time," he promised.

Evelyn shook her head at the memory. "This is the last time," she repeated.

A melodic chime sounded, mingling with the tap of Evelyn's steps and the creaking of door hinges. A whimper caught in her throat as Hex and Snip stepped from the shadows of the door. Their skin was several shades lighter, and their eyes were dull and unfocused. Sweat darkened their hair and traced their hollow cheeks. Evelyn's lip trembled as she took in their broken state.

No longer able to hold herself back, Evelyn ran forward and dropped to her knees before them.

80

Snip's stare stayed lost in the distance, while Hex's dull eyes fixed on hers. Evelyn shook her head, wrapped an arm around each child, and pulled them to her chest. Her sobs echoed in the silent hall, and Caelum's heart cracked a little more. "Never again," she promised.

The soft tap of approaching steps was like a sharpened stick poking a bear. The echo of footsteps drew Caelum's ire; fury burned deeply in his eyes and vibrated through his body. He whirled on Hadeon and spat the venom-laced words, "This is it. The last. I will not let you continue this torture."

Hadeon chuckled, and Dorrin and Casimir smirked. "You agreed to the trials, Caelum," said Hadeon.

"Yes, I did. My first mistake. But I will not continue to make it. It has been years and, aside from a divided soul, you have found nothing to show corruption or malcontent that will lead to the destruction of this Realm. This is over."

Hadeon's eyes darkened. "You think you get to decide when this is over?"

"Actually, he does," Lytos interrupted.

Hadeon's lip curled in disgust at Lytos's presence. "We have not received the answer to the question that has been asked."

"No, you haven't even tried, have you?" Caelum demanded. "Instead, you have been using them to conduct your experiments! You have broken the contract, Hadeon, and therefore you will be sent into exile."

Hadeon smiled and wagged a finger. "I am afraid you are wrong. We posed the question and conducted our experiments to find the answer."

Caelum clenched his fists, his body glowing with intent as he slipped into a fighting stance. Lytos's warm hands gripped his shoulders.

"He's right," Lytos conceded, before addressing the room. "However, if Caelum says this is done, it is done. The contract was signed by us all, and this is its fulfillment. He has catered to your whims for years. You have received all the answers that you will have. You may have wormed your way out of exile, but you will leave his kingdom." Lytos tilted his head with a dark smile. "Unless you wish to challenge me again, Hadeon?"

"That won't be necessary."

Caelum and Lytos turned to find Nalik strolling merrily toward them with a small, elderly woman in tow. Long silver hair fell down her back, accenting the soft blue robes that billowed as she walked. Her eyes were pure white, as if she were blind, and yet when she turned her attention to Caelum, he shifted uncomfortably. "Nalik, who is this?" Caelum asked.

Evelyn stood and tucked the twins behind her protectively. Recognizing the woman, her eyes widened in surprise, and she closed the space between them, gripping her sons' hands. "Themis! How have you been?"

CHAPTER FIFTEEN

One by one, the kings dragged their attention to the frail woman at Nalik's side. Their eyes widened.

Themis smiled, and her face folded into innumerable wrinkles. "I am well, dear. How are you? Are these your beautiful boys?" she asked, smiling down at the pair.

Hex eyed the old woman, his head tipped to the side in obvious inspection. Snip's lip trembled as he tucked himself behind his mother. Evelyn nodded enthusiastically, oblivious to the glares and mumbled curses from the men behind her. "Yes! This is Hexius and Snip. Come on boys, say hello. This is mommy's dear friend Themis. She helped me when I was pregnant with you two."

Snip wrapped himself into his mother's skirt and looped his hand through his brother's. Hex wondered at his brother's reaction but took a protective step in front of him. Themis smiled at the display and held out her hand. "Do you mind if I touch you?" she asked.

Hex looked to his mother for guidance. At her nod of encouragement, he took a step toward the elderly woman. "Okay," he rasped.

Themis's eyes crinkled in sorrow. "Don't you worry. I will not hurt you."

Hex snorted at her words. Realizing what he had done, his eyes widened in disbelief at his own bravery.

Themis chuckled and settled her hand on his sweaty head. Her eyes fluttered shut as her lips moved in a soundless chant. Hadeon, Dorrin, and Casimir took curious steps forward while Lytos and Caelum exchanged a worried glance. Nalik rocked back on his heels with a smug smirk.

Themis furrowed her brow, and a soft breeze filtered down the hallway, rustling their hair and pulling at their clothing. When she opened her eyes, they had darkened to a slate grey. Pressing her lips together, she wagged a finger in Hadeon's direction. "You are a terrible, terrible man. The things you have done to these children are unacceptable! They were a gift from the Stars themselves and you dare to treat them as less! If I were young enough to trifle with the Eternals…"

Hadeon cleared his throat and lifted his chin. "I am seeking answers. Protecting this Realm. Their birth was unnatural."

Themis narrowed her stormy eyes. "All you had to do was ask, truly ask. Not dig around in their souls like a mucker. You could have sought me out as Nalik did, and you would have had your answers You chose neither of these."

"Your existence was believed to be a myth. You should be locked away with the other Old Ones," Dorrin said.

"I would hold your tongue, young one. Most of the Old Ones were locked away for a reason, and I would love to show you why."

Dorrin paled under the power of her words.

Themis turned her strange stare to Hadeon. "The trials are straightforward. Take a matter of hours to finish and, if Nalik is to be believed, you have taken over twenty-four hours and have not found the answers you seek. Tell me, is it because you are searching for something that is not there?"

Hadeon's cheeks colored in anger. "I have done as the contract stated. I have searched through their bodies, minds, and souls to find out if their existence endangers the Realm."

"And why would you think such things about children?"

"They are t-t-twins," Hadeon sputtered.

Themis arched a brow. "And?"

"Twins do not exist. Eternals excised them from our race. They were created unnaturally. It is only right that we question their destiny."

"Their destiny has been shoved from its path because of you!" Themis snapped. "You added misfortune and pain to their lives—etching their souls in despair—because of your own ignorance. The Eternals did not take them from your race. That is a terrible story that bored men tell themselves to excuse their own dreadful deeds. The Eternals cursed several families to slow their procreation of evil. Twins have always been a rarity in this Realm, but that does not mean it cannot happen. Especially when *I* make it so. These trials have ended, as decreed by me: Themis of Old. If you commit another act of malice toward these boys, I will have no choice but to take action."

The room fell into shocked silence. Their souls hummed under the direction of someone from whom they were all derived. Snip peeked out from behind his mother's dress. Suddenly overtaken by courage, he leapt from his hiding spot. He padded across the stone floors and flung his arms around Themis's legs.

"Thank you," he whispered. Themis smiled and patted the boy's head, but her gaze never left Hadeon.

"Fine," Hadeon agreed. "We are done. For now. But keep in mind, Caelum, this is not over. They have a dark destiny, and I will find out what it is before they drag us all to the Underworld." Smoke filled the room and when it cleared, Hadeon, Casimir, and Dorrin were gone.

Lytos waved his hand in front of his face to dissipate the lingering smoke. "Always so showy, they are. It's a tragedy they wield the power that they do."

Solastra stepped from behind her brother's back with a bored expression on her face. "Well, that was annoying."

"Solastra! I can't believe I didn't notice you before." Evelyn laughed, hugging her friend tightly.

"Things were a little crazy for a moment there, no hard feelings."

"I hate to be a terrible bother, but would you mind it terribly if I spoke with Hex and Snip for a bit?" Themis asked.

Evelyn hesitated, but finally nodded. "Alright. Why don't we go out to the garden? It's a nice day and the boys could use some sun."

"I would like to speak to them alone," Themis clarified.

Evelyn paled. Solastra laid a hand on her shoulder and gave her a reassuring smile. "It will be alright, Evie. Themis wouldn't hurt them."

No. Don't take them. Not again! Evelyn shook herself free of her terrible thoughts. "Right, of course. I'll have some snacks sent out. Hex, Snip, why don't you take Themis to the garden? Show her your favorite spot." Evelyn waited for their hesitation, for the boys to beg her to come with them. Instead, she found herself disappointed. The boys smiled as they each took her hand to lead her from the hall.

"That is a good thing, Evelyn. They feel safe with her," Solastra consoled.

Evelyn swallowed and blinked through the burn of tears. "It's really over," she whispered, leaning into her husband when she felt his encroaching warmth. "It's really over."

"Yes," he said with a smile.

"Thank you, Nalik."

Nalik shrugged. "It was Solastra, really. Though what took her so long is still a mystery."

Something flashed in his sister's eyes but was quickly hidden with a smile. "I had my own affairs to attend to. Though, if I had known…"

Evelyn patted her friend's arm. "It is over now. I just want to move on."

"Then move on, we shall. What kind of snack should we get those lovely children of yours?"

Nalik, Lytos, and Caelum watched the girls walk down the hall with linked arms. "You know this isn't over, don't you?" Lytos asked.

Caelum nodded. "Yes. But let's let her have this win, at least for a little while."

Chapter Sixteen

Themis basked in the sun's warm rays as the twins led her through the beautifully blooming garden. At her right, Snip chattered away, telling her of all of his likes and dislikes, his favorite flowers, and the ones he thought smelled like day-old feet. He had chuckled after that, bringing a smile to Themis's weathered face.

"You want to tell us something important, don't you?" Hex asked.

Themis peered down at the quieter twin and felt a squeeze in her chest. She didn't see like others did and never had. She saw more than just the flesh on their bones and features upon their faces. She saw what was beneath it all—destiny and fate interwoven within the colors of their auras and the battle of light and dark that waged within their very souls. What she saw littered throughout Hex brought a deep sorrow into her that permeated her ancient bones.

"I might. Does that worry you?" she asked.

Hex's face scrunched together in thought before he shook his head. "No, I like it when people say what they really want to."

"Let's sit over there!" Snip announced, releasing Themis's hand and disappearing. His giggle echoed in the air as he reappeared at the bubbling fountain and attempted to copy the pixies' dance.

Themis laughed and settled herself onto the surprisingly soft stone bench. "Uncle Lytos made this bench for my mom when she was pregnant with us," Hex explained. "He gave the stones a special charm. He said she was out here all the time and sitting on a hard stone would hurt her. So, he made this."

"That was nice of him."

Hex shrugged and looked worriedly between the ancient woman and his brother, unsure of what to do.

"Snip, would you come here for a moment?" Themis asked.

Snip waved goodbye to the dancing pixies and appeared at her side.

"Have you been doing that long?" she asked.

Snip lifted a shoulder. "I don't know."

Themis arched a brow. Hex rolled his eyes and pulled his brother to sit on the ground at Themis's feet. "We started doing it a few months ago. But I told him not to do it in front of other people," Hex chided.

Snip flushed. "Sorry, Hex. I forgot."

Hex sighed and bumped his shoulder against his brother's. "That's okay. Just be more careful next time."

Themis watched the exchange in fascination. In all her years, she had never seen a set of auras pulse and change as theirs did. When one aura was out of sync, the other instinctively fed it the necessary emotions until they were back on track. Raw power was woven between every thread in their bodies, enhancing their natural auras. *I see what Hadeon was so curious about.*

"I wouldn't be too upset. Pixies rarely interact with humans. It just shows how special you two are." The boys flushed under the praise. "Have you boys been able to do anything else?" she asked.

Snip looked to Hex for guidance, and at his nod, answered. "We can open portals and make things appear. I got a cake one time. A really weird cake. I don't think it was from here."

"Where was it from?" Themis asked.

Snip scrunched his nose. "I think it was a goblin's party. It tasted like trash."

Hex rolled his eyes. "I told you: stealing is bad."

When Snip rolled his eyes in return, looking exactly as his brother, Themis couldn't hold back her laughter. "That is a lot for children of your age."

Snip puffed up at the compliment. "We are going to be the strongest in the Realm."

Themis smiled. "I have no doubt. Is there anything else?"

"Nope. Not yet."

"Why do you say 'not yet'?"

Hex shrugged. "I just feel it."

Themis nodded at the wise words. "And you are being careful, yes?"

The twins nodded.

"Very good. Now I am afraid I must tell you something very adult-like. You might not understand it now, but I need for you to keep it in mind and ponder over it every once in a while until you do. But you mustn't tell anyone else."

Hex and Snip stared blankly. "Not even Mom and Dad?"

Themis frowned. "I am afraid not. It will have to be a secret between just us."

Hex shook his head. "We don't lie."

"That is very good," Themis praised. "Alright then. You may tell them. But only if they ask. Is that fair?"

Hex and Snip exchanged a glance. Themis watched as their auras wove in and out of each other. "Alright," they agreed.

"One day, in the future, you two are going to be in a terrible situation where you have to choose between what is right and what is wanted. You must always choose what is right. Do you understand?"

"No." they chirped, Snip's voice an echo of Hex's.

Themis reached down and took their hands in her own. "It is a terrible burden to place on such young souls, but I am afraid even I cannot alter the path you are on to the one you were supposed to take. The life you lead will not be fair. It will be hard, and cruel, and at times crippling, but you are strong and you must always stick together."

Snip frowned. "We're brothers. We always stick together."

Themis smiled and kissed the tops of their hands. "That is right. I am sorry I cannot help you."

Hex shrugged. "That's okay. We can help ourselves."

"I hope we are not interrupting," Evelyn called.

Themis winked at the twins. "Not at all. In fact, it is time for me to leave."

"Already?" Hex asked.

Themis tapped a finger to his nose. "I will see you again," she promised. "Both of you. But I have been gone far too long as it is."

"Are you sure?" Evelyn asked, as she, Solastra, and the remaining kings joined them. "It has been so long since we last met, and I thought this time we could spend more time together. We brought snacks and tea."

Themis rose from the bench. "I am afraid so. I have many things to do and not much time to do it. Solastra, are you coming with me?"

"Yes, Themis." Solastra pulled Evelyn into a hug. "I will be back. I promise."

Evelyn nodded against her shoulder. "You'd better."

Solastra pulled away and stepped to Themis's side. "Caelum, if you wouldn't mind, dear," Themis urged, waving at the empty air.

Caelum blinked at the sudden order and flicked his wrist. When a pink portal opened, his brow furrowed. "I don't…"

Themis chuckled. "It wasn't you, dear. Portals know where I wish to go on instinct. Come, boys, give this old woman a hug." Hex and Snip threw their arms around her legs and squeezed tightly.

"Bye, Themis," they echoed.

Themis smiled and booped each of them on the nose. "Mind your parents."

The twins nodded and raced back to the fountain while Evelyn and Caelum said their goodbyes. "Visit anytime," Evelyn urged.

Themis waved as Solastra helped her toddle to the glittering pink portal. "Oh, and Evelyn?" she called over her shoulder.

"Yes?"

"Congratulations on the pregnancy. I promise this one will go smoother." Themis winked.

The portal closed with a soft pop, leaving Caelum and Evelyn reeling with the new revelation.

CHAPTER SEVENTEEN

Chilling flames engulfed his paralyzed body as the large, looming figures stared down at him. They wore amused smiles, fascinated. The pain continued to build, and he could barely breathe. Snip had already crumpled to the ground beside him, eyes wide and empty; his body twitched, his mouth open in a silent scream.

The largest figure stepped closer, a fanged smile breaking his lips. If Hex had control of his body, he could reach out and drag his tormentor into the pits of hell with them.

"They all bow eventually," the tall one declared. "This will all be over if you just give in."

The desire to cave in was tangible as the metallic taste pooled in his mouth. Mustering his last bit of strength, Hex shook his head. The man smiled, as if this was his plan the whole time, and snapped his fingers. The pain snaked its icy fingers around Hex's throat, digging into his soft flesh. Everything went dark.

Snip thrashed on his bed. His head whipped from side to side as pleas for reprieve spilled from his dry, cracked lips. Blood-tinged sweat stained the sheets. Heat seared his flesh and his arms were gripped by invisible hands, pinning him to the mattress.

"Please," he whimpered. "No more."

His pleas grew louder and more frantic with every moment. Servants filled the halls, between the two young master's rooms as cries Finding the late-night happenings curious, the servants huddled together, spewing whispered theories and rumors.

Another shrill scream split the air and a door burst open. A sleep-disheveled Caelum and Evelyn raced down the hall toward the group of wide-eyed servants. "What's happening?" Caelum demanded.

The servants huddled closer together, fear leeching from their pores. "The boys. Their screams woke us," a young man finally said. Caelum recognized him from the stables.

Caelum gritted his teeth and took another step forward. "And no one thought to check on them? Or wake us?"

The servant's lips trembled beneath his scrutiny. "Sor-sorry, Your Majesty."

"Leave. All of you."

Painful moans rumbled beneath the doors, the twins' distress rising. "Get Hex and bring him to Snip's room," Evelyn tossed over her shoulder as she slipped inside Snip's bedroom.

Caelum sent a withering glare at the slow-moving servants, which sent them scurrying away. Inside his son's dark bedroom, his heart squeezed painfully when he found the young boy softly crying, his knees hugged tightly to his chest.

"Hex? Are you alright if I come over there?"

Hex looked up with watery eyes and held out his arms. Caelum rushed to his bedside and pulled him onto his lap. "It's alright," he cooed, rocking him softly. "Would you like to get changed and go in with your brother?" Hex sniffled and nodded his head against his father's shoulder. "Alright then."

Evelyn rushed across the cool floor and crawled into Snip's bed. Snip cried out, fighting against the sheets that tangled his body. "It's alright, Snip. Mommy's here." She closed her eyes and placed her palm against her son's heated forehead. Snip's cries dissolved into whimpers and finally silence as his eyes opened.

"Mommy?" he croaked.

Evelyn smiled and pulled him into her arms. "That's right, you're safe now."

"I'm cold," he whispered.

Evelyn snapped her fingers, bringing the muted glow of a light orb into the room. "Let's get those wet clothes off. I'll get some fresh clothes for you and change your sheets."

Snip was silent and distant as he changed his clothes. His eyes held shadows of haunted thoughts that were much too mature for a boy of only six. "Alright, honey. Come here." Evelyn held out her arms and Snip walked into them, never complaining when she lifted him into bed and settled herself behind him.

"I love you, Snip," she whispered. Snip sighed, his soft, even breath already filling the space between them as he curled into her.

Just as Evelyn began to doze off, the click of the door closing rousing her consciousness. Caelum carried Hex—freshly clean and changed—into Snip's room and laid him on the soft mattress before climbing in behind him. Evelyn opened her eyes at the shifting mattress and smiled at Hex. "How are you doing, my little dove?" she asked.

Hex sniffled and shrugged. "I'm okay. Is Snip sleeping?"

Evelyn peered down at the boy nestled into her chest and nodded. "He is."

"Oh."

Evelyn's smile turned sad at his disappointed tone. "Here, come closer. I am sure it will give him comfort to know you are here."

Hex scooted closer and rested his head against his brother's back. A relieved breath poured from his lips and fanned his neck. "Hex?" Snip groggily whispered.

"Yeah?"

Without opening his eyes, Snip turned from his mother and rested his forehead against his brother's. Caelum chuckled as both boys instantly began to fill the air with soft snores. "Never fails," he whispered before leaning to kiss each goodnight.

Evelyn nodded into the darkness and ran her hand through the silky strands of Snip's hair. "How long do you think it will last?"

Caelum settled himself back against the pillow. "How long will what last?"

"The nightmares. Isn't there anything we can do?"

"There isn't an answer for that. I have asked everyone with any knowledge of the mind, and no one has an answer. The best we can do is continue to support and love them through it and hope that it fades with time."

"We have to protect them, Caelum. And the next one. We can't let Hadeon do what he did to them."

"Never." Caelum vowed. "Nothing will ever destroy what we have built. Time may take us away, but nothing will take Hex and Snip away. They are going to be amazing older brothers. You just watch."

Evelyn smiled at the thought as she snuggled deeper into the mattress and let sleep take her. She was oblivious to the countdown that loomed above her, the seconds ticking by…

Chapter Eighteen

Eight months later

The sun bathed the kingdom in its warmth as soft, fluffy clouds trailed lazily across the striking blue sky. The gentle breeze carried the scent of newly blossoming flowers and chased away the heat. It was as though one of the bedtime stories their mother had always told them had come to fruition.

Only this wasn't a happily ever after kind of day and their mother wasn't telling them a story in her garden. It was her funeral. She wasn't laughing with them in the grass; she was laying inside a glass coffin, atop a rainbow sea of eternal flowers. Her midnight-colored hair was neatly arranged over her shoulders, where it softly brushed against her clasped hands. Like a princess waiting for true love's first kiss to break the curse, she slept. But this wasn't a fairytale and no matter how many kisses she was given, she would never wake again.

Hex cursed the Stars for allowing such a beautiful day to exist. Anger spread like venom through his body with every pump of his heart. His stomach felt heavy and his heart ached, as if his body were filled with rocks. Snip sat beside him, silently sniffling but uncharacteristically quiet, for the first time that he could remember. Another wave of emotion washed over him as a soft whimper followed by a deep cooing caught his ear. Hex shifted in his chair. His father had arrived and, with him, their new sister.

Hex glared at the white bundle his father carried. "It's her fault," he mumbled.

Snip sniffled and turned to follow Hex's gaze. "That isn't true, Hex. She's a baby."

"If they didn't have her, mom would still be here."

Snip didn't hesitate before shaking his head. "It was supposed to be this way."

Hex snapped his teeth together and swallowed an angry retort. "You don't know that."

Snip turned to his brother with empty eyes. "Yes, I do. And you do too; you just won't admit it. There is nothing we could have done. Themis said some things in life won't make sense. This is one of those times."

"How can you say that? Don't you even care? Mom is *dead,* Snip. She's never coming back."

"I know that. But I will not blame our baby sister for that. She couldn't control what happened any more than we chose to be what we are."

Hex burned with rage. He never fought with his brother, or anyone, for that matter. He was the calm one. The level-headed one. And yet, today, he found himself lost in the depths of his anger and grief.

"It's beautiful, isn't it?" a mourner murmured from somewhere behind him.

Hex frowned at the thought. Death was an ugly thing that left nothing but devastation in its wake. Those left behind were forced to live the rest of their days with gaping, festering wounds on their souls and when they too inevitably passed on, the cycle would begin again.

Hex turned in his chair and glared at the golden-eyed woman who had spoken. "What's so beautiful about it?"

The woman silently stared, and Hex shifted uncomfortably in his chair. With a compassionate smile, she leaned forward and placed a warm hand over his. "To live a life so full of love and to leave it better is what we all hope for. Your mother was an incredible woman who brought three precious souls into this world. She wouldn't want the anger you feel to darken the light within your soul. The flowers you see blooming around you are a sign that your mother is with you. Always. Cherish it."

The woman looked over his shoulder and patted his hand once more before leaning back into her seat. With her words buzzing in his mind, Hex examined the tomb in a new light. She was right; it was beautiful. In a cruel, heart-shuttering sort of way.

While their father struggled with the loss of his love and the reality of being a single father to three, Lytos had taken control of the funeral arrangements. He worked late into the night constructing the beautiful pergola that would entomb their mother, and one day, their father, for all time. Utilizing his affinity with earth, he had called forth the deep roots of the willow tree and wove them together, recreating her life story within the lines and filling the gaps with carved flowers, trumpet vines, and Evelyn's favorite, morning glories. Hex's eyes roamed over the beautifully constructed art and felt the wetness of tears down his cheeks. Displayed on the walls was the greatest love story he had ever been told. The one of his mother and father.

A sharp elbow to his ribs ripped him from his inspection. "What?" he snapped at Snip.

Snip tipped his head. "Dad is talking to you."

Hex blinked to clear away the burn of tears and looked up at his towering father. He looked different. The last twenty-four hours had drained him of the glow that Hex remembered. "Yes?"

Caelum cleared his throat and squatted to eyelevel. "I have to say a few words. Would you mind holding your sister?"

Hex stiffened, his mouth opening to scream no, when Snip adjusted in his seat so that their shoulders touched. As it always did, his brother's proximity soothed the mix of emotions and gave him the strength to nod.

A thankful smile lifted their father's lips as he carefully placed the bundle in Hex's arms. "I'll be right back and then we can leave," he promised, but Hex wasn't listening.

The moment his sister was placed in his arms, something undefinable rippled through him. He stared down at the watery-eyed child and the world dissipated. Her lip quivered as she stared up at him, as if she was just as lost in this new world as he was.

"I'll always protect you," he vowed.

Snip leaned forward and placed a finger against her flailing hand, smiling when she squeezed it tight. "Your big brothers won't ever let anything happen to you."

CHAPTER NINETEEN

One Year Later

Hex was trapped; strapped to a table with three pairs of merciless eyes staring down at him. Red hair waved like a flame in the wind as the brown-eyed man stepped forward. His teeth gleamed, ending in sharp points. *"I wish I could say this wouldn't hurt, but that would be a lie and our contract prevents that,"* he murmured, rolling up his sleeves.

Strapped down beside him, Snip whimpered.

Hex glared at the man. "One day, I'm going to do everything back to you," Hex spat.

The brown-eyed man threw his head back and laughed. "I'd like to see you try."

Hex jerked upright in bed, his body shaking from the icy sweat soaking through his night clothes. His heart hammered so fiercely he grabbed his chest, afraid it was going to leap out and leave him forever trapped within his mind.

A sliver of light broke through the darkness, accompanied by the soft creak of his door. Hex swallowed the saliva filling his mouth as fear stole his breath. A shadow stretched from the doorway, growing until it threatened to swallow the room. Hex bit back a whimper when the shadow drifted toward his bed. A relieved breath rushed past his lips as a familiar shape followed the shadow through the door.

"Hex?" Snip whispered. "Are you awake?"

"Snip," he breathed. "What are you doing in here?"

Snip scurried to the bed, the pale moonlight illuminating the wet tracks streaking down his cheeks. "Did you have it too? The nightmare?"

Hex cleared his throat and tossed the blankets back. "Yeah. Do you … do you want to sleep in here?"

Snip sniffled and shrugged. "Only if you need me too."

Hex looked over his brother's flushed, tear-stained face and quivering lip and mirrored his brother's lackadaisical shrug. "Yeah. That would be nice."

Snip wipe his nose against his sleeve and climbed quickly into bed. Slowly, the pair gravitated toward one another, their skin mirroring the other. "You're soaked," Hex whispered.

"You are too," Snip tossed back.

Hex sighed as he slipped from the bed. Silently, he padded across the smooth floor and pulled open a dresser drawer. A bitter feeling filled his stomach. The nightmares have plagued him for so long he could easily move throughout his room, even on the darkest night. A disgusted sound passed his lips as he withdrew two fresh sets of nightclothes and a blanket before moving back to the bed.

"Here, we need to change, otherwise we will get sick."

Snip sniffled once more and crawled to Hex's side of the bed. "What about the sheets?"

Hex lifted the hand with the blanket and waved it slightly. "I'll just put this down and then we can sleep."

Snip nodded, as if his brother's words were the wisest that he had ever heard. Hex pulled back the heavy comforter and threw the extra blanket over the sodden sheets. A frown pulled down his lips as he flipped the pillows. "Do you think it'll always be like this?"

Snip shook his head. "No."

They changed in silence, each lost in their own misery, and climbed into bed. Hex reached down and pulled the blankets up to cover them before laying down to face his brother. "How are we going to fix it, Snip?"

Snip chuckled. "You're the smart one. Shouldn't I be asking you that?"

Hex shook his head. "You're smart too."

Snip let his brother's comment go unanswered and lifted his attention to the large window where the moon lit up the night sky.

Silence blanketed them until their eyelids grew heavy. Snip watched his dozing brother, his breath even. "Should we tell Dad?"

"No," Hex murmured, without opening his eyes.

"Why not?"

Slowly, Hex opened his eyes. "Because if we did, the Realm would be at war."

Snip frowned. "Dad said the Realm was already at war."

Hex sighed. "Shadow war. Which means it isn't an official war. There can't be any active strikes against anyone."

"But then…"

"Exactly. Get some sleep, Snip."

Snip sighed and snuggled deeper into the plush pillows as the door cracked open once more. Wide-eyed, the brothers sat up, a relieved sigh escaping their lips as a tiny figure toddled into the room.

Hex climbed from the bed and rushed to gather his sister in his arms. "Evie, what are you doing in here?"

"Sleep," she said with a yawn.

Hex chuckled and carried her back to the bed. "Alright, but only for tonight." Evie giggled and nestled herself next to Snip.

"You came to sleep with us?" Snip whispered, kissing the top of her head.

"Yes."

Hex shook his head with a smile on his face and pulled the covers over his siblings. "Goodnight, Evie," he said, kissing her forehead.

"Night, night."

The sound of Evie's even breathing filled the still room. "Hey, Hex?" Snip whispered.

Hex released a rushed breath. "What?"

"Thank you."

Hex's brow furrowed as he squinted over his sister's head. "For what?"

"For protecting me. Back then and now."

"I didn't protect you, Snip."

"You may not think so, but you did. I crumbled each time, but you stood tall, even when I knew it hurt, and because of that, they took some of it off me and put it on you."

"Don't think about that anymore. It's all over. Just get some sleep."

"Okay … hey, Hex?"

Hex groaned. "What?"

"I'm going to make them pay. All of them. I won't let them do what they did to us to Evie. I'm going to find a way that won't hurt Dad or Uncle Lytos and then I'm going to do everything they did to us to them."

Hex let his brother's words go unanswered for a while before whispering, "Go to sleep, Snip."

Long after Snip's soft snores echoed around the room, Hex lay awake, watching him sleep. As the night wore on and sleep finally began to weigh on his eyes, he pulled Evie tighter against his chest. "I won't let you darken your soul, Snip. So, I'll do it for you. For both of you," he vowed.

CHAPTER TWENTY

Four Years Later

"**B**ut I don't want to go." Evie sniffled. "I want to stay with you and Snip."

Hex looked up from the shoe he was sliding onto her foot and flinched. Large, red-rimmed, spring green eyes stared back at him. If it weren't for the tears shimmering in them, Hex would swear they were his father's. Hex released the foot he held and wiped the tears from her plump cheeks.

"Don't cry, Evie. It's going to be fun. You will get to play with kids your age and make friends and learn new things. Doesn't that sound exciting?"

Evie's lip began to tremble. "You and Snip don't want me here anymore?"

Hex shook his head. "That's not it at all. We love having you here with us. We're going to miss you terribly, but we want you to make some friends. Besides, it's only for a couple of hours."

Evie's trembling stopped. "Do you promise?"

Hex smiled and tapped a finger on her nose, inciting a giggle. "Promise. Now, are you ready to go to your first day of school?"

Evie shrugged, hesitated, and finally nodded.

Hex stood and held out his hand. "Alright then, let's get going."

Evie jumped from the chair and slid her tiny hand into his larger one. "Is Daddy coming?"

"He has a meeting with Uncle Lytos and Uncle Nalik, so Snip and I are going to drop you off. But he will pick you up this afternoon."

"Oh."

Hex squeezed her hand reassuringly and led her out of the frilly pink bedroom. "Snip! Let's go! Evie is going to be late on her first day!"

"Why are you yelling?" Snip asked from behind them.

Hex jumped as Snip's breath whispered over his neck. "Stars, Snip! What did I tell you about sneaking up on me like that?"

Evie squealed with a mixture of laughter and short-lived fear. "You scared me, Snip."

Snip smirked at his brother and knelt in front of his sister. "I'm sorry, Evie. But I have something for you."

Evie's enormous eyes grew impossibly wide. "A present? For me?"

Snip jerked back in mock offense. "Of course, for you! Did you think I would let you go to school without a good luck charm? What kind of brother would I be?" He shot his twin a quick glance.

Hex glared back while Evie bounced on her toes, oblivious to the ensuing rivalry. "What is it?" she asked excitedly.

Snip suppressed a smile. "Now Evie, is that what we say when someone has a gift for us?"

Evie pursed her lips and shook her head. "No."

"What do you say?"

Evie's lips twitched with growing excitement. "May I please have my present?"

Snip beamed. "Of course, you can, sweet Evie. Here you are."

Snip pulled a hand from behind his back to reveal a plush pink bunny and bopped her on the nose with it. Evie's green eyes brightened as her smile became radiant. "It's so cute!" she declared, bouncing on her toes as her earlier distress faded away and the room burst with her unfettered happiness.

Snip stood and held out a hand. "Are you ready for school now?"

Evie bobbed her head and squeezed the plush bunny to her chest. "Yup."

Snip sent his brother a victorious grin. Hex rolled his eyes, his lips twitching with a smile, and snapped his fingers. "Let's go. We don't want you to be late."

Evie skipped toward the pale pink portal her brother created. "I always get the pink ones," she giggled.

Hex and Snip exchanged a smile as the same memory fluttered to the forefront of their minds as they followed their excited sister through the portal.

"Come on, Evie! We are going to go on an adventure," Hex cooed at the waddling toddler, gesturing to the portal.

Evie stepped to the side, staring in curiosity at the swirling grey mass and immediately broke into tears. "But I no want to."

Panic welled in the brothers at their sister's sudden and complete meltdown. Snip knelt by her side. "What's wrong, Evie? You like traveling through portals."

"It's scawry," she sniffled.

"But why?" Hex asked.

"Dark."

As realization slowly dawned, Hex snapped his fingers and pink swirled into the grey, until it washed it out entirely. "Oops, I forgot, Evie. That wasn't your portal—this is."

Evie looked up with a trembling frown. "It's pink!" she cheered, her fear suddenly a distant thought.

Evie hesitated when the beautifully built white building came into view.

"Do you think this is a good idea?" Snip whispered to his brother.

Hex swallowed through his own doubt and nodded. "She needs friends her own age."

Snip snorted as the bright yellow door opened and a petite blonde woman stepped out. "You must be Evelyn," she said with a smile.

Evie took a step back toward her brothers and nodded. "Her name is Evie," Hex snapped. "She likes to be called Evie."

The woman blinked rapidly at his sharp tone and offered a shaky smile. "Of course. Why don't you come inside, Evie? We have a lot of other children that would love to play."

Evie looked up at her brothers with a trembling lip. Snip smiled and grabbed her free hand. "Come on, Evie. Let's go look around."

The woman frowned, her eyes bouncing between the twins. While Snip ignored the looks and led Evie into the building, Hex smiled darkly at the woman and leaned in close to whisper, "Everything you've heard is true." The woman gasped. Hex chuckled and followed his siblings inside.

"Isn't it nice, Evie?" Snip asked.

Hex swallowed his pout. Unfortunately, his brother was right. The school building was an open concept with enchanted walls that depicted a spring day—complete with large fluffy clouds and a softly glowing sun that drifted across the room. Bookcases lined the walls, stuffed with books and toys. A charmed doll twirled as it sang a song, teaching some kids about shapes and colors, while others sat in a neat circle listening to a story.

A child sat off to the side by herself. Hex frowned as an uneasy feeling shifted beneath his skin. She was a delicate girl, smaller than the others, with honey-blond hair, bright blue eyes, and a red nose.

Evie pulled on his shirttail, drawing his attention. "Why is she all alone?" she whispered.

Hex pursed his lips. "I'm not sure."

The woman who had greeted them eyed the little girl uncomfortably. "That's Seraphina. She just started here earlier this week and keeps to herself."

Evie started toward the other girl. "She's going to be my friend."

"Evie—"

Snip caught Hex's arm. "Let her go. We will pick you up later, Evie."

Evie paused and raced back over to hug her brothers. "Bye," she chirped before sprinting away.

Silently, Hex and Snip watched as their sister coaxed the other girl out of her shell. "Come on, people are staring," Snip urged.

Hex shot the group of teachers a withering glare before turning on his heel.

Chapter Twenty-One

One Week Later

"Evelyn!" Caelum bellowed into the forest. His heart was on the verge of leaping from his chest when his call went unanswered once more. After arriving at the school and finding the children were left alone and that Evie wasn't even there, fear had threatened to swallow him whole. His mind stuttered to think while Hex and Snip sprang into action. Caelum had watched in surprise as their bodies took on a strange glow and a thin strand had appeared, shot into the forest, and quickly vanished. That strand was now gone.

"I'll find her," Snip vowed and disappeared.

Caelum rushed through the woods, his head on a swivel as he scanned every bush, fallen log, and towering tree.

"Don't worry, if Snip said he'll find her, he will," Hex promised.

Caelum looked at his eldest, finding his calm demeanor disturbing. "Hex—"

"She's that way," Snip interrupted, his sudden appearance startling his father.

Caelum smiled at his youngest son and patted his head before racing in the direction he had indicated.

"Are you alright?" Snip asked.

Hex shrugged. "Doesn't the air feel strange?"

Snip's brow creased. "I guess so."

Hex shook his head. "Forget about it. Come on."

They broke through the thicket of trees just in time to catch their father scooping Evie into his arms as an older woman stepped forward to shield a petite blonde child. Snip hissed a breath, noticing the same dark aura as his brother.

"Would you like to share what has happened here?" Caelum asked.

Hex was vaguely aware of the conversation his father was having with the strange girl's mother. *Seraphina,* he reminded himself. The girl Evie had immediately declared would be her friend on her first day of school. She was small, smaller even than Evie, which was a sight to see. She had long, blonde hair and enormous blue eyes. Outwardly, she gave off the air of innocence, but Hex knew better. Something was wrong.

"That's Sera. I told you about her daddy. She's my friend." Evie giggled, pulling Hex back to the conversation at hand.

"Yes, you did, didn't you? How silly of me to forget." Caelum smiled and tapped his finger on his daughter's nose.

Snip watched Evie slip from their father's hold and race over to the other little girl.

"Sera, this is my daddy. Isn't he tall?"

Seraphina nodded, her eyes wide. "So tall," she whispered.

Snip shifted from foot to foot. His skin itched as if a thousand ants were just beneath its surface. "Something's wrong here," he whispered.

Hex took a step closer to his brother. "It's the girl."

"What is she?"

Hex shook his head and plastered on a smile when Evie looked in his direction. "I have no idea, but we need to keep her away from Evie."

"Agreed."

"Would you like to meet some of my friends?" Caelum's question made both of his sons stiffen and the girl's mother whimper.

"That sounds fun. Can Evelyn and Cleo come too?"

Caelum's smile grew. "Of course. Would you like to come, Cleo?"

Four tireless days had passed since Seraphina and her adoptive parents had come to the castle. Four days of hushed adult conversations. Four days of Hex and Snip uneasily watching the playing girls, waiting for the moment Seraphina would become the threat they knew she was.

They didn't know whether to feel relief that nothing had transpired or dread that it meant something greater was building. In the last four days, they had shadowed the girls during their run through the gardens, game of hide and seek in the library, and sat through excruciating hours of doll play.

"Maybe we were wrong," Snip whispered as the girls changed their dolls' dresses.

Hex thought about it for several minutes. Keeping his eyes glued to Seraphina's laughing face, he shook his head. "I don't think so. However, I don't think she is a threat in her current state."

"What do you mean?"

Hex pinched the bridge of his nose in frustration. "I don't know!" he exclaimed.

The adults chatting at the nearby table went silent as they turned in their direction. "Hex?" Caelum called. "Are you alright?"

Hex cleared his throat. "Yes, sorry."

While his father seemed content with his answer and turned back to the discussion, Lytos kept his worried eyes on the boy. Hex shrugged, motioning to where Seraphina and Evie sat twirling their dolls and shrugged. Lytos nodded with a tight smile and held Hex's gaze for another moment before turning back to his tablemates.

"Well, that wasn't very smooth." Snip chuckled.

"Oh, shut up. You—"

"With her abilities, we can find those responsible for the soul experiments," Lytos said, his excitement at the thought brightening the slow glow around his body.

The adults' whispered conversation was easily picked up by their superior hearing, and the brothers paled as they looked at one another. "Hex." Snip trembled.

Hex shook his head and forced a smile. "They won't get to you Snip. I promised."

"It has to be her choice. I will not stand by and let a child be used." Nalik's voice rumbled with a warning.

"Then we ask her. Evelyn said that she has a special tie to the Realm. That she hears it crying out because of something dark. If she is that connected, then we can use her to find out who has started this shadow war."

"And where will she go? Hadeon is already banging at your door, demanding that the trials begin again. What do you think will happen when they find out about her?"

The blood rushed from Snip's face, making him waver on his feet at the mention of the trials. Hex grabbed his shoulder to steady him and pushed an extra pulse of calming energy through their shared connection. "Breathe, Snip. They are just talking."

"Then we don't let them," Lytos insisted.

Everyone's attention shifted toward Lytos. "What?" Caelum asked.

"I'll take Seraphina. I can have several homes cloaked with indifference spells. They will never find her. If they happen to find out about her and go looking, they won't be able to take her. No one but those with my blood can enter those homes without my permission."

Nalik and Caelum shared a meaningful look, and Lytos rapped his knuckles against the tabletop. "Alright, it's settled then." He rose and smiled at Hex and Snip before kneeling beside the playing girls. "Seraphina?"

Seraphina looked up with a smile. "Yes?"

"Would you like to help us?"

Seraphina frowned. "Help you?"

"Yes. Help me and everyone and everything in the Realm."

She pursed her lips. "You are going to help the Realm?"

He smiled. "I would like to—very much."

Seraphina looked to Evie for approval., and Hex clenched his fist at his sister's nod. "Okay," she whispered.

Lytos beamed, filling the air with warmth and a soft, glowing light. "I was hoping you would say that."

CHAPTER TWENTY-TWO

Evie sighed, another piece to a never-ending, exaggerated stream that had left her mouth as she gazed out the large window. Snip dropped his head onto the library table and Hex pinched the bridge of his nose. She heaved another sigh.

"Evie," Snip pleaded. "Please stop."

Evie looked over at her brothers with wide, innocent eyes. "Stop what?" she asked.

Hex narrowed his eyes. "You *know* what. That sighing you have been doing all afternoon. We told you that you could be in here, but you had to be quiet and do your lessons. You have done neither. Now, come over here and get some work done."

Pouting, Evie climbed off the window seat and stomped over to the table. "But I'm sad, Hex."

"Why are you sad?"

"Because Sera is gone, and she's my only friend. Now Daddy won't let me go back to school." Evie finished her mini tirade with an undignified plop into her chair and a violent crossing of her arms.

Snip kept his head down, fearing the tantrum his smile might summon. "We're your friends too."

Evie rolled her eyes. "UGH! You don't get it!"

"Good job, Snip," Hex mumbled.

Snip sighed and straightened in his seat. "Then explain it to me. Are we not good enough to be your friends?"

"You *can't* be my friend."

Snip jerked back with a hurt expression. "Why not?"

"Because you're my brother."

Snip looked at his twin helplessly. "That's not true. You can be friends with us. Right, Hex?"

"No, because you have to like me. I'm your sister," Evie protested.

Hex snorted. "I assure you that is not why we keep you around."

Her curiosity piqued, Evie sat up. "Why do you keep me around, then?"

Hex closed his book and slid it across the table. "We keep you around because you are our *best* friend. Because we love you and we want to see you grow and become someone great."

Evie's eyes widened. "I'm your *best* friend?"

"Of course." Hex smiled.

Her eyes shifted to Snip. "Am I your best friend?"

Snip beamed and leaned forward, curling his finger to draw her closer. Eager for a secret, Evie leaned forward. "You're my best, *best* friend," he whispered.

With an excited gasp, Evie slipped from her seat and ran to stand between her brothers. "Okay, we can be friends." She smiled, hugging them both.

Close one, Snip mouthed. Hex shook his head and squeezed his sister, causing her to squeal.

Suddenly, a knock sounded on the door.

"Come in," Hex called, running his fingers along Evie's sides and sending her into a fit of giggles. Two cooking aids rushed into the room, carrying trays filled with snacks and drinks. Evie's peals of laughter slowly came to a halt as she noticed their strange behavior. As they artfully arranged the trays along the center of the table, the two women kept their heads bowed and eyes averted. Their hands twitched with nervous, frantic movements.

"Is something wrong, Evie?" Snip asked, snagging a finger sandwich from the closest tray.

Evie looked from one quivering servant to the next before turning back to her brothers. "Why are they scared of you? Are you mean to them?"

The room went still. Sweat dotted one of the women's brow as dishes clattered roughly against the table. Hex fought the urge to roll his eyes as they exchanged a frightened glance. Snip cleared his throat. "You can go."

Thankful for the reprieve, the servants raced from the room and slammed the door behind them. Hex sighed and dropped back into his chair. "What makes you think they fear us?"

Evie lifted a shoulder. "Because no one ever looks at you. When we were in the garden last week, Bottie ran away as soon as she saw you."

Snip frowned. "Who's Bottie?"

"She's the lady that takes care of the plants. They sing to her. Did you know that?"

"I didn't know flowers could sing."

Evie nodded. "Yup, and she tells them stories. I listen sometimes. But whenever you come to get me, everyone runs away. Were you mean to them?"

Snip shook his head. "No, we weren't mean to them."

"Then why do they do that?"

"Because sometimes people are afraid of those different from themselves," Hex explained.

"Differences? You guys aren't different."

Snip released a snort. "Some people think so."

"But you look the same. Not all the same. Sera said she couldn't tell you apart, but *I* can tell you apart."

Hex smiled and selected a finger sandwich for his sister. "Yes, you can. Here, eat."

Evie nibbled on the sandwich. "Are they mean to you?"

Snip shoved a cookie into his mouth and shook his head. "No, they aren't mean to us. Not anymore. Ouch!"

Hex glared as Snip rubbed his shin.

"What was that for?" Snip snapped.

"For opening your mouth. You shouldn't talk with your mouth full."

"That's true, Snip, you shouldn't. It's gross," Evie chirped.

Snip popped another cookie in his mouth and stuck out his tongue, sending Evie into another round of giggles.

"I asked Daddy," she added casually.

Snip sucked in a breath, choking on his cookie, and earning several extra hard back slaps from Hex. "You did what?" he gasped.

"I asked Daddy why everyone is scared of you."

"What did he say?" Hex asked.

"He told me to go play." Evie set her sandwich down and looked at her brothers. "Someone was mean to you guys. That's why you have bad dreams and why you stay away from everyone."

"Evie…"

"It's okay. You don't have to tell me. But I won't let anyone be mean to you anymore, because friends don't let bad things happen to friends. And neither do sisters. I'm going to grow big and strong so I can protect you guys." Sandwich in-hand, Evie moved back to her seat and began doing her lessons while her brothers stared after her, mesmerized by the vow their sister had made.

Chapter Twenty-Three

Evie wandered halfheartedly after the giggling pixies. Hex and Snip were gone again. Off on some important mission for their father. Something they couldn't share with someone her age.

"Why do you have to leave again?" Evie asked.

Snip looked at his twin with sad eyes. Hex rolled his but offered her a smile. "Father needs our help. We won't be gone for long, but we need you to be a good girl and listen to your teacher."

"But I'm a big girl," she whispered through a sniffle.

Hex smiled and brushed the tears from her cheeks. "Of course, you are. But even big girls don't get to know everything. Be a good girl, Evie."

Evie kicked at a rock and sent it flying into a bush. Frightened, a bunny burst from the brush and scampered into the woods. Evie's lips quivered. "I'm sorry," she called after it. The pixies paused and fluttered back to her side. "I'm not sad," she assured them. "Or lonely."

The soft chirp of pixie talk bubbled in the air.

"I know they'll be okay, but I miss them when they are gone." After another round of chirping, Evie's eyes widened. "Really? A special friend? Is she close?"

The pixie twirled in the air sending a soft cloud of glitter to rain down onto the grass.

"Okay, then." She smiled.

The pixies surrounded her in a flurry of bright colors, earning another giggle, and flew off into the woods. Not one to be left behind, Evie pushed her little legs to follow. She was surprised when the muffled roar of water began to echo in the air.

Her little heart pounded by the time she reached the dancing pixies. Surprise pulled what little air she had left from her lungs. "Wow," she gasped. "This is beautiful." A waterfall of purple rushed from high in the mountain and splashed into a large pool. The rich color of the water paled as it lapped against the shore, revealing the bright green fish playing inside.

A teenaged girl, or part of one, lay out on one of the large, flat, sun-warmed rocks with her lavender hair fanned out. Her fins trailed through over the edge. The soft swish of her ombre tail brushing along the water accented the steady rush of water. Evie smiled in wonder as the dew drop shaped scales caught the sunlight and sent the shimmer of rainbows into the waterfall.

"HI!" Evie called, waving her hand frantically in the air. "I'm Evie. Who are you?"

The girl jumped at Evie's unexpected greeting and toppled into the water. Evie shrieked, panic closing her throat as she ran toward the shoreline. She wasn't the best swimmer, but she couldn't let the girl die. Just as she steeled herself to jump into the water, the purple-haired girl popped out of the water. "Naiya," she whispered.

"What?" Evie asked.

"My name is Naiya."

Evie frowned, then smiled as her mind caught up. "Oh! Hi Naiya! Sorry I scared you. I thought you were going to drown. I'm glad you didn't." Evie beamed. "I like your hair."

Naiya's brow furrowed at the compliment. "My hair?" she repeated. Evie nodded as Naiya lifted the sodden strands. "Thank you," she breathed. "I've never had anyone say that before."

Evie's eyes widened. "Really?"

"Really."

Silence filled the space between them, breeding uncertainty. Evie rocked from side to side, her eyes roaming the glistening waterfall of purple and settling on the glittering pink flowers.

"What are those?" she asked.

Naiya followed the direction of her pointed finger and smiled. "Those are special flowers. Here, I'll show you." Naiya dove beneath the water's plum-colored depths only to reappear at the water's edge to pluck one of the acorn-shaped flowers. With a couple of quick strokes of her glittering tail, she floated just inches from Evie. "Come closer," she urged.

Evie hesitated. "My brothers said I shouldn't trust strangers."

"Oh, okay." Naiya set the bloom on the shoreline and swam back to the center of the pool. "Go on," she urged.

Evie rushed forward, her childlike curiosity outweighing the warnings of her brothers. Plucking the flower by its stem, she inhaled its citrusy scent and sighed. "Smells so good!"

"Now, peel off a petal and rub it between your hands," Naiya instructed.

Evie frowned but did as she instructed, an excited squeal piercing the air as bubbles began to form between her palms. "It's soap!"

Naiya giggled. "Yes. Neat, isn't it?"

"Oh, yes." Evie agreed as she dipped her hands into the water and washed the bubbles away.

"Evie, can I ask you a question?"

"Okay." Evie settled herself on the ground and stared at her new friend.

"How did you find this place?"

"The pixies."

Naiya glared at the balls of light and shook her head as the bell-like twinkling of the pixies' giggles reached her ears. "Silly pixies," she mumbled.

"Can I ask you a question?"

"Okay."

"What are you? You look like a girl, but you have a tail."

"I'm a pagaeae."

"What's that?"

"A water sprite. This spring is my home and I guard it."

"All the time?"

Naiya smiled and nodded her head. "All the time."

Evie's brow furrowed. "But what are you guarding it from?"

Naiya's smile dimmed. "I'm not protecting it from anyone. I'm protecting what is in it."

"Oh."

"I know that makes little sense, but I am afraid I can't share anything else."

Evie shrugged, tearing the grass from the ground. "That's okay."

Naiya watched the girl curiously. "Evie, is something wrong?"

Evie sighed, her little shoulders rising and falling in dramatic fashion. "I'm not allowed to know what my brothers are doing."

"Why not?"

"Because Daddy sent them to do something that they can't talk about."

Naiya tipped her head. "Adults do that sometimes."

"Why?"

"To protect you, of course."

"Wh—" Evie hesitated.

"What is it?" Naiya pressed.

"What if I want to protect them?"

"What do you mean?"

"People are mean to my brothers. They say terrible things. Some wicked men hurt them when they were little and now they have nightmares. They think I don't know, but I do. People don't pay attention to me because I'm a kid, but I still hear what they say, even if it is whispered. I promised them I would protect them, but how am I supposed to do that if I don't know what they are doing?"

Naiya pursed her lips in thought. "Alright then, I suppose you will have to get stronger."

"But how do I do that?"

"Have you found your ability yet?"

Evie sighed once more. "Yes, but it won't help."

"Why not?"

"Because I can only make sad people happy."

"But Evie, that is a great power!"

Evie scrunched her nose in disbelief. "It is?"

"Yes! And a rare one at that. With your ability, you can keep your brothers' spirits up. When they are frightened, you can make them brave and give them strength when they are ready to quit. You are a very special girl, Evie. You don't need to have any other ability because you can change things already."

"How?"

"If people are sad or mean to your brothers, then change the way they feel. Help others see in them what you do. If you can do that, you can change the Realm."

Evie's eyes widened with understanding. Scrambling to her feet, she waved frantically at the girl and raced for the tree line. "Thank you, Naiya!"

Naiya smiled. "Where are you going?"

"To change the world so I can protect my brothers."

"Evie, wait!" Naiya called.

Evie stopped and turned back. "Yes?"

"Will you be back?"

"Of course. You're my friend."

Naiya watched the little girl disappear into the woods with a smile on her face.

A large shadow stretched across the grass and blocked the sun from gracing her skin. "You know that isn't how it will end," a gravelly voice said.

"I know. But let her dream, Senan."

Chapter Twenty-Four

Several years later

"Come on, Evie! It's a picnic, not a damn ball," Snip groaned.

"Leave her alone," Hex sighed, punctuating his words with the flipping of pages. "Your voice is grating on my ears."

Snip pursed his lips and crossed his arms. "We should have left by now. She won't tell us where we are going. She wants it to be a *surprise*." Snip sneered at the word as if it was the most disgusting thing someone could recommend. "And yet, she takes half the morning getting dressed."

Hex growled and snapped the book shut as the burn of anger filled his limbs. Closing his eyes, he began the familiar pattern he used to restore his calm. Inhale, exhale. The room shifted as Snip's impatience grew, his foot tapping a staccato upon the floor. Inhale, exhale. *Tap, tap-tap, tap, tap, tap-tap-tap.* INHALE, EXHALE. Hex peeled open his eyes as his relaxing breathing technique faltered. Snip rested his hip against a nearby table, his face twisted into a frown. His grey eyes were as dark as a brewing storm. Hex shook the worry away and began his process again.

Inhale, exhale. *Tap, tap, tap, tap-tap-tap, tap, tap-tap.* Hex flinched at the inconsistent tapping.

Inhale, exhale. Snip's popping knuckles added to the tapping of his foot.

Inhale—

"Ugggghhhhhhh," Snip groaned.

"ENOUGH!" Hex snapped. Carelessly tossing the book onto the side table, he lurched out of the oversized armchair and stomped over to his smirking brother. "Is this amusing to you?"

"Yes, actually. It is."

Evie walked into the room with a smile that quickly faded. "Hey!" she snapped. "This is supposed to be *my* day. So you two put on your fake smiles and follow me!"

Hex continued to glare when Snip turned on his heel with a smirk and followed their sister. Hex took a deep breath before shaking his head and following his sister outside. "Where are we going?"

"It's a secret," she giggled in a singsong voice.

"How are we supposed to get you there if we don't know where to go?" Snip asked.

"We follow the pixies, of course." Evie giggled.

"Follow the pixies? Pixies don't use portals," Hex explained.

Evie rolled her eyes. "We are walking!"

Both brothers stopped at the edge of the woods. "Like, the whole way?"

Evie turned back with a mischievous smile. "Don't tell me you two are afraid of a little hike."

Hex and Snip exchanged a long glance before looking back at their sister and simultaneously shrugging. "Of course not. Let's go," Hex murmured.

"*Follow the pixies,*" Snip grumbled. "I'll follow the damn pixies and do it better than you."

"I'd like to see you try," Hex challenged.

Evelyn chuckled under her breath but followed her brothers through the woods, her mind somewhere far away as she struggled under the weight of still unanswered questions. Pixies and sprites danced through the air, the soft clapping of their wings a tempting melody. As her mind drifted away in search of answers, she admired the simple beauty surrounding them.

"Evie? What's wrong?" Hex asked.

The concern in his voice snapped her attention away from the pixies' dance. Evelyn looked up and found her brother's beautiful face pulled down in a frown. For a moment, she contemplated lying, then remembered how terrible she was at it. "Do you ever wonder what death is like?"

Hex sucked in a harsh breath. "Why would you ask something like that? Have you seen something?"

"What's going on?" Snip asked, slowing to match their pace.

Her brothers, though mirror images, were just that: mirrors of each other. Though they reassembled the other perfectly, they could not be more opposite. Hex was straightforward in everything that he said and did. He wielded knowledge and logic like the incredible weapons that they were. Snip was more laid back and whimsical, preferring to use tricks and games to get what he wanted. While he was just as smart, he used his knowledge to make his games livelier. Both were deadly when put to the test. "Nothing," Evelyn said. Still, she couldn't seem to tear her eyes away from Hex's.

"It is not *nothing*. Evie just asked if I thought about what death was like," Hex countered.

Snip frowned. "Why would you wonder about something as boring as that?"

Hex glared at his twin. "What is wrong with you?"

With an exasperated sigh, Snip ran a hand through his hair. "Always so serious, Hex. She just asked a question. One that many think of every day. If there was something to it, she would have said so. Right, Evie?"

Evelyn nodded, afraid that her voice would give her away.

"See? Now come on," Snip said.

"This is not over, Evie," Hex promised.

Evelyn forced a smile. "Of course not."

"Are you sure you don't want us to portal you there?"

Evelyn giggled at Snip's apparent exhaustion. "It would do you good to get some actual movement out of your body. Just because you can jump around the Realm with a single thought doesn't mean you should."

"And why not?" Snip asked, a smile curving his lips.

"Because exercise is wonderful for you. When you jump around through portals, you grow lazy and you miss out on the surrounding beauty."

Snip rolled his eyes, a move that Evelyn had dubbed his signature move. Never in her thirteen years could she remember Hex doing such a thing. He called it "childish."

"Why do I need to notice the beauty of the world when you are here?" Snip asked, draping one of his long arms around her shoulders. "Besides, when you portal, you get to enjoy more of what you want in a day. We have spent all of this time walking aimlessly through the woods to get to some magical lake, when we could have brought you straight there and enjoyed it longer."

Evelyn shook her head. "Fine," she said with a dramatic sigh. "When it is time to go home, you can use your portals."

Snip tipped his head back with a boisterous laugh. "I get it now, you sneaky little rabbit. You may have wanted to walk here, but you had no intention of walking back. How terribly *me* of you."

"That's enough, Snip. You do not need to rub any more of your bad habits off on our poor sister," Hex warned, though his smile softened any malice in his words.

Snip pressed a hand to his chest in mock horror, his other falling from Evelyn's shoulder as he prepared to square off with his brother. "Me? Bad habits? Outrageous!" he proclaimed.

Evelyn laughed as her brothers fell into a familiar rhythm of bickering. "Oh, you two," she giggled. "Imagine the things you could accomplish if you worked *with* each other instead of against."

Snip's grin grew as he shifted his attention to their sister, while Hex's stoic expression held strong. "Always so wise." Snip said, snickering. "Strange, given you are the youngest."

Evelyn shook her head. "Yes, me being wise is the strangest part of our family."

In fact, the strangest thing was the pair that stood in front of her. Twins were unheard of in the Realm and, before they arrived, thought to be impossible. The tales of what they had gone through since their birth haunted the shadows of their home.

Over the years, Evelyn had overheard snippets of the whispered stories. Some were so horrifying that she wondered how much was truth and how much was fabrication. The need to know more had brought her to her father. The few times she had found the strength to ask, he had given her a sad smile and sent her off on another silly task. She had asked the twins only once. The crippling pain that had creased their beautiful faces had etched itself into her mind and ended any further inquiry.

Evelyn shook the sad memory away and focused on the here and now. Snip grinned as he made casual digs at Hex's stone-like expression—comparing him to the giant gargoyles that watched over the castle grounds. When Hex refused to engage his brother, Snip turned his attention to Evelyn, his expression immediately falling into one of faux exhaustion and toddler-like moodiness.

"*Eevviiiee…*" he whined. "Are we almost there? My legs are going to fall off and then how much fun will I be?"

Hex snorted. "As if you were ever fun."

Snip frowned. "Evie, Hex is being mean."

Evelyn pinched her lips together and shook her head, attempting to hide her smile and swallow the chuckles that shook her chest. "Calm down, we are nearly there," she promised.

Snip groaned. His steps grew heavier as he slapped them against the ground. "You said that an *hour* ago."

"Don't be ridiculous. We have only been walking for half that," Hex corrected.

"Dammit Hex—"

"We're here!" Evelyn interrupted.

This time, both Hex and Snip frowned as they looked around at the tree. "This is … nice?" Hex said.

Another laugh escaped as Evelyn pulled back the twisting tree branches. "No, silly. Here."

Chapter Twenty-Five

Evelyn smiled as her brothers gasped. Their wide eyes sparkled with amazement at the wonder and beauty that was displayed before them. They walked to the center of the naturally created circle of trees. Plush, vibrant green grass sponged their steps as they turned to take in their surroundings. Large flowers with rainbow petals lifted their silken heads to brush against their fingertips. Black stones circled the space and swallowed the surrounding light, trapping it inside and making the stones glitter against their darkened shadows.

"How did you find this place?" Snip asked.

A rosy blush warmed Evelyn's cheeks as she tucked loose strand of hair behind her ears. "I get bored sometimes and the pixies keep me company. One day, they led me here. It's been my favorite place ever since."

Hex kissed his sister's cheek. "Thank you for sharing it with us, Evie."

Evelyn shrugged. "You're my brothers. Of course, I wanted to share it with you guys."

"If this is supposed to be a picnic, where is the food?" Snip asked.

Evelyn laughed at her brother's insatiable hunger, and Hex rolled his eyes. "Follow the pixies," Evelyn instructed.

Snip dropped his head back and groaned. "Again?"

"It's my day, remember? You two have been gone for ages and today is supposed to be about what *I* want to do. So, Snip, you follow the pixies to the Rowan wood and gather some for a fire. Hex, you find out where they hid the snacks they made. They like to make a game out of it, so no cheating."

"And what are you going to do?" Hex asked.

Evelyn beamed as she strode to the center of the circle and spread herself out in the plush grass. "I am going to lie here and watch the clouds roll across the sky."

"Well, that doesn't seem fair." Snip frowned.

"I never said it would be." Evelyn laughed. "Go on now. I'm feeling peckish."

The brothers exchanged a glance and sigh before leaning down to kiss their sister's head. "Be good," Hex called back as the brothers split off in different direction, venturing after the pixies.

Evelyn smiled as she watched them go. "Today is going to be perfect." Closing her eyes, she released a contented sigh and basked under the sun's warm rays.

Snip had followed the bouncing green and yellow orbs for far too long before realizing that they had been leading him around in a large circle.

"Crafty bugs you are," he chided. The orbs tittered and fluttered to his eye level to squeeze his cheeks. Snip shook his head at the mischievous pixies and shooed them away. Satisfied with the conclusion of their game, the pixies shot off into the distance to swirl around an ancient towering rowan tree.

"Alright then," Snip sighed.

Sweat poured from his body by the time he had finished gathering the wood and began his trek back to Evelyn. Mumbled curses streamed from his lips at the insanity of her no magic promise.

The sound of lapping water echoed in the forest's silence, drawing Snip's attention to his parched throat. He hesitated briefly before stepping off the path. Before too long, the trees separated, and a large oasis opened up before him. Lilac water slapped gently against a shoreline made up of multicolored stone. A towering purple waterfall rained down near white droplets that cascaded into the pool.

Snip ventured forward as his eyes greedily drank in the wondrous sight. A flash of bright color drew his eye from the waterfall to the shore. A smile crested his face at the sight of the swirling green fish. Setting the bundle of rowan wood on the ground, he crouched beside the water and swirled his finger in the foam, chuckling when the fish began to follow.

"That's not very nice," chided a feminine voice. "You shouldn't tease the fish."

Snip's head snapped toward the sound. His body tightened into a fighting stance as his eyes scanned the area.

"Oh, calm down. I'm not going to hurt you."

The voice was closer now—too close. Snip turned back to the water and stumbled back at the sight. A girl lazed in the water a mere foot away. Her skin was luminous, as if she swallowed the sun and its glow radiated from her. Light purple hair swirled amidst the plum-colored water. Her hair matched her eyes and the water in which she swam.

"Who are you?"

"I'm Naiya, and you are?"

"Snip."

Naiya's eyes flashed. "Are you now? How very interesting."

"I don't see how. What are you?" Snip asked, none too kindly.

"A pagaeae. What are you?"

Snip's brow furrowed in thought. "I'm not sure."

"Don't worry. Few people do."

"Why are you in there?"

Naiya giggled, the sound reminding him of the popping of bubbles. "Because I am a spring sprite, of course. And this is my domain."

Snip swiped his tongue over his chapped lips and dipped his hands back into the warm water with a frown. "You wouldn't have anything to drink, would you?"

Naiya smiled, revealing her glittering white teeth. "What I have, I'm afraid you can't drink. It wouldn't be good for you."

Snip shrugged and stood. "Well, Naiya, it was nice to meet you, but I have a sister to get back to."

"Travel safe, Snip, and tell Evie I said hello."

"How do you know Evie?"

"She comes here a lot. She likes the flowers." Naiya pointed toward the waterfall, surrounded by flowers.

Snip looked over and smiled when he saw the glittering blossoms. "I'm sure she does. It was nice to meet you, Naiya."

"You, as well. If you pass through those bushes, you will be back in no time."

"Thanks."

"Don't worry. You can make it up to me someday."

Snip turned, intending to tell her he wouldn't be back, but she had already disappeared beneath the plum depths of the spring. Shaking his head, he lifted his bundle of kindling and started in the direction Naiya had recommended.

CHAPTER TWENTY-SIX

Hex sighed under his breath as he followed the chattering pixies through the dense forest. "You find this amusing, don't you? Those with the power of Travelers forced by their younger sister to walk!" The sound of twinkling bells rang out, and Hex shook his head. "Hilarious, truly. Now, how about you show me the way to the berries instead of walking me in circles?"

The pixies transformed into resplendent green orbs and shot off into the distance. Hex groaned but spurred himself into a sprint. He panted, his heart pounding in his chest. How long had it been since he had run? *Maybe Evie was right*, he thought begrudgingly.

The pixies came to a sudden stop in the distance, and Hex's racing heart leapt for joy. As he came to a stop, he bent at the waist, his hands resting against his knees as he struggled to catch

146

his breath. Blood roared in his ears when he stood, a frown pulling down his sweaty features.

"What's this?" he demanded. The pixies glowed vibrantly as they wove themselves around a bush nestled between a set of towering, wide trees. "You were supposed to bring me to Evie's favorite berries."

The pixies hovered and released a string of incomprehensible chatter.

Hex shook his head and placed his hands on his hips. "I don't understand what you're saying."

The pixies swarmed the bush once more, ruffling the branches and lifting the leaves to reveal plump, pink berries. Hex pursed his lips in surprise. "Alright then, thank you." He smiled, and, again, the pixies froze mid-flight. "What?" he pouted. Twinkling bells sounded once more and Hex felt a blush heat his cheeks. "Whatever," he mumbled. He knew he didn't smile often. Evie told him every chance she got, but the pixies didn't need to *giggle* when he did.

Hex shook his head and looked around for a place to store the berries. "Alright, don't tell on me," he whispered with a wag of his finger. The pixies bobbed closer as he twirled his hand above a patch of earth. Thick blades of grass grew tall to brush against his fingertips and, with a snap of his fingers, wove themselves into a neat basket. Hex smirked at his creation and lifted a finger to his lips. "Our little secret, okay?"

The pixies bobbed their agreement and fluttered away.

"Wait! I don't know how to get back!" Hex called. When the pixies continued into the distance, Hex shook his head. "So much for guides." Reaching down, he plucked the basket from the ground and knelt before the bush to gather the sparking berries. "What in the..." Hex sat back on his heels and pulled another berry free from the branch. His eyes widened as another instantly grew in its place.

"Fascinating, aren't they?"

Hex dropped the basket on the ground and twisted on his heel to face the voice. A tall, silver-haired man of average build stood a few feet away with a smirk fixed on his timeless features. His eyes, though they glittered the same silver, had slithering black lines curling amidst his irises. His eyes seemed to pry deeper into the depths of Hex's soul with every passing second. Unease curdled Hex's stomach. "Who are you?"

"Senan."

Hex frowned as the name itched *something* in his mind. "I know that name."

"Do you?" Senan asked.

Hex glared at the smirking man and searched through the endless pages of his mind. His jaw clenched as he fought to keep the blood from draining from his face. "You are one of the three Eternals."

"Correct!" Senan beamed. "You're a bright one, aren't you?"

Hex swallowed through the dryness in his throat. "What are you doing here?"

Senan snorted and swaggered closer. "Silly question. After all, I helped create this place. I think I deserve to visit every once in a while."

Hex slowly nodded and rose to his feet. "Yes, but the Eternals disappeared centuries ago. What are you doing here, *now*?"

"I supposed that is a fair question." Senan sighed and swept his eyes around their surroundings. "I guess you could say I got bored."

"You got bored?"

"Yup," Senan said, popping the p. "Immortality is rather boring. Especially when you have to spend it with the same two people."

Hex narrowed his eyes. "What do you want?"

Senan's gleaming white smile reminded Hex of the wolf from his mother's bedtime stories. "Straight to it then. I like that about you, Hex."

"You don't know me."

Senan dropped his head back in an outrageous laugh that sent the slumbering birds fleeing from the trees. "Of course, I do. I know everyone. It's my … job."

Hex shifted under Senan's slithering gaze, his unease growing. "So?" he urged, eager to be done with the conversation and run far away from the Eternal.

Senan watched him for another silent second before relenting. "There is a change coming to the Realm, and I want your help to stop it."

Images of Evie and Snip in danger passed through his mind. "What kind of changes?" Hex asked.

"Someone is trying to release a … power into the Realm that they have no right to mess with. I need you to stop it."

"Why don't *you* stop it?"

Senan pursed his lips into a displeased pout. "Rules were created long ago that prevent such things."

"Alright then, I'll humor you. What kind of power is being released into the Realm?"

"One that is too much for the average human to hold. But then again, you're not average, are you?"

Irritation pulsed through Hex's veins. "What does any of this have to do with me? Go to the Seven Kings. That's why you created them, right?"

"Corruption runs deep. I need *your* help. But don't worry. I'll give you something in return."

"What?"

A predatory grin curved the Eternal's lips. "Anything you want. Eternals can do many things, as you know, and many things you don't."

"HEX!"

Snip's desperate plea ripped through the air, thick with his anguish. "I have to go." Hex's eyes flared with panic as he darted into the woods.

"Remember what I said, little twin," Senan called after him.

Branches lashed the tender flesh on his face and hands as he used the pull of his brother's soul to guide his steps. Young roots snapped beneath the pounding of his feet. Animals fled from his path and raced into the forest, driven by their own panic. The sky darkened under the turmoil of their emotions, slashing the sky with lightning, and rumbling the clouds with the angry clap of thunder.

Blood roared in his ears as the familiar break in the trees appeared. His brother's pleading voice broke through the small tree barrier, bringing him barreling into the beautiful oasis. The world froze as Hex's brain struggled to comprehend the sight that was laid out at its center.

"Snip?"

Chapter
Twenty-Seven

"Alright Evie, it took a while, but I think we have everything now. Are you ready to get a fire going?" Snip asked as he trampled through the glittering bushes. Confusion knit his brow when she did not answer. "Evie?" he called, his smile fading as his steps faltered. The bundle of rowan wood slipped from his grasp. There wasn't anything particularly unnatural about the way his sister lay. Nor were there any concrete signs to indicate that anything was amiss. And yet, every small step that he took brought another knot to his twisting stomach. "Evie," he croaked. Desperation began to claw its way up his throat.

With another step, his heart was ripped open in his chest. Evie lay just as they had left her, with her dark hair fanned out around her like a darkened halo and her hands resting at her sides. She lay silent and still, her eyes closed as though she were sleeping, oblivious to the sun's heated rays falling upon her pale skin.

"HEX!" Snip bellowed. Crumbling to his knees, Snip gathered his limp sister into his arms and pressed his hand against her chilly cheek. "Evie, Evie, please. You have to wake up. Evie!"

Hex burst into the clearing with mud clinging to his clothes and blood seeping from the jagged scratches lining his face. "Snip? What is it? What's wrong?"

A tortured moan ripped from Snip's throat as he turned back to Evie's limp body in his arms. "Come on, Evie," he cried.

"Snip!" Hex snapped. His brother looked up with watery eyes. "What happened?" he pressed.

Snip shook his head. "She won't wake up, Hex. Why won't she wake up?"

The clearing spun before Hex's eyes as the blood rushed from his face and pooled in his feet. "No," he whispered. Stumbling on suddenly unsteady feet, he dropped to his knees opposite his brother and pulled Evie into his arms. "Evie." Silence. "Evelyn!" he snapped, tapping his hand against her cheek. "Evie, dammit, *look at me!*"

Snip's agony ripped at his chest. His hands twisted in the dark strands of his hair. "Fix her! Hex, you have to fix her! Please." Lightning slashed the sky, unleashing a vicious downpour around.

"Shut up, Snip! Come on, Evie. Wake up."

"Hex," Snip groaned, pacing helplessly across the dampening ground.

Hex shook his head as he shifted Evie fully into his arms and stood. "Let's go."

Snip paused. "Where?"

"To Father."

Snip shook his head. "We have to fix Evie!"

Hex shot him a heated glare. "We will. Let's go."

Snip watched in stunned silence as his brother disappeared into a portal he never saw him create. His wonder was quickly replaced with burning fear for his sister as he slipped through the swiftly closing portal. A frown furrowed his brow as he stepped into a room he had never seen before. His father, Lytos, and Nalik hunched over a table with serious expressions on their faces.

"Father," Hex pleaded.

"I think this is the only way. If we can locate one—" Caelum turned, confused at the intrusion, to find his drenched sons and his limp daughter in Hex's arms. "Hex? How did you get in here? What's going on? Why are you carrying Evie? Is she okay?"

Hex shook his head, his voice coming out in a desperate croak. "We don't know what happened."

Caelum paled, and Nalik and Lytos exchanged confused expressions. "What do you mean?" Caelum managed.

"She's not breathing!" Snip shrieked. "Fix her!"

In the blink of an eye, Caelum flew across the room, taking his daughter from Hex's arms and laying her on the nearby couch. "Evie, wake up."

"What happened?" Lytos asked, rushing to the couch.

The twins shook their heads. "We went to get wood and snacks and when we came back—" Snip started.

"You left her?!" Caelum raged.

Snip blinked at the fury in his father's voice. He could count the number of times his father had raised his voice at any of them on one hand. "Evie wanted us to get wood and berries."

"Get the healers," Caelum ordered. "Now!"

Snip was gone in an instant and returned the next with three disheveled-looking passengers. The eldest, a balding man draped in wrinkles, bent at his waist, heaving.

"Fix her!" Snip demanded.

The healers fixed their eyes on Evie's still body. "We need the room."

Caelum paced the hall in front of the closed doors while Nalik and Lytos focused their attention on the twins.

"Tell us again," Nalik requested.

Hex flexed his jaw, anger rearing its head as their sympathy quickly turned into an accusation. Thoughts fluttered in the air like fallen paper. "Is there something on your mind, Nalik?"

Nalik narrowed his eyes. "What are you talking about?"

A humorless smile lifted Hex's lips. "I can see what you're thinking. You think we did this? That we hurt our sister."

Caelum stopped pacing.

Lytos's jaw dropped. "That's not true, right Nalik?"

"You can't be serious?" Snip asked darkly. "Evie is our life. We do everything for her. Always have."

"Tell us again," Nalik demanded.

"Evie wanted to spend the day together. Since we have been busy with our studies and *missions*, we haven't gotten to spend much time with her. She led us through the forest, to an oasis she had discovered. She sent me for snacks and Snip for wood. Told us to follow the pixies. We did. Snip found her, called for me, and here we are."

"And that's all that happened?"

"No," Snip interrupts. "I met a pagaeae at the waterfall when I stopped for water."

Nalik pursed his lips in thought before turning back to Hex. "And you? Any other encounters?"

"I met Senan."

Shock rippled through the hall. "When? Where?" Caelum demanded.

Hex fixed his father with an empty stare and snapped his fingers, opening a sizzling portal. "See for yourself."

The grinding of hinges ended their conversation and pulled their attention to the slumped healers. "Your Majesty, we tried everything. Her soul … it's gone."

Chapter Twenty-Eight

One week later

"Look again," Caelum ordered.

The healers shifted from foot to foot, uncertainty tightening their faces and twisting their hands. "But we have. Several times. Your Majesty, I am sorry but—"

"LOOK AGAIN!" Caelum roared.

The healers whimpered under their breath as the crushing weight of his power threatened to buckle their knees. A warm hand clapped down on Caelum's shoulder, tearing his burning gaze away from the cowering healers.

"Caelum, they did everything. Everyone has. But even Nalik cannot find a soul once it has been taken," Lytos murmured.

Caelum shook his head, his fingers pulling at his oily hair. "No, that's not true. If they keep looking, then we can find it. We can fix this."

Lytos's face pinched in sorrow. "It's over."

"Lytos, I can't…" His words trailed off as the inevitable end fought to penetrate his mind.

"It's been a week, Caelum. We have turned every rock and brought in every healer and soul searcher we could find. Solastra told you, Caelum. Then you stooped to letting *Dorrin* try, and he failed. I am sorry, my friend, but this is the end."

"I told you there would be consequences," Hadeon interjected.

Burning with hate, Caelum lunged toward Hadeon, only to come up short when Lytos wrapped an arm around his waist an inch before contact. The room temperature plummeted, dropping heavy snowflakes from the ceiling. "I suggest you watch your tongue," Nalik warned.

Hadeon glared, the effect dampened by the frantic, chilled clicking of his own teeth. "I am sorry, Caelum. But you must see things from my side."

A growl rumbled through Caelum's chest.

"You've been warned," Lytos said. "One more comment and I'll let him go."

"He can't touch me. We have the bond," Hadeon said haughtily.

"He can't, but we can," Hex promised as he and Snip strode into the room.

Hadeon smiled as he looked over his two favorite subjects. They had grown in the years since the trials. Their auras, as plain as day to his eyes, were rolling with unspent energy. "Hex, Snip. How lovely to see you again! Have you missed your Uncle Hadeon?"

Hex tilted his head. "That depends. How have you been sleeping?"

Hadeon's eyes widened. "I don't know what you're t-t-talking about," he sputtered, dropping into his seat.

Lytos looked at his nephews with frightened awe. Over the last week, he had been forced to watch Caelum crumble beneath the weight of his loss for the second time. Only this time, he feared the anger and disconnect was here to stay.

But that wasn't what had planted fear into his heart.

A charcoal glow leaked from Hex and Snip, following them like a menacing shadow and cloaking them in raw, untapped power when they stopped. Lytos had watched them do the impossible, as if it was as natural as breathing. They weren't just Travelers or Healers; they were so much more. Their moods shifted the weather and tainted those unlucky enough to be caught within their web of influence. Objects of all shapes, sizes, and uses materialized at a snap of their fingers. Information poured into their minds by simply placing a hand upon a book.

Lytos cleared his throat, drawing their empty eyes. "What brings you here?"

Snip frowned when his body shivered from Nalik's freezing temperature. He clapped his hands, dissipating Nalik's magic. As the room warmed, the snow melted, disappearing without a trace. Nalik masked his surprise, but not before Lytos noticed. "We want to know what the next step is."

Caelum's jaw clenched as he forced his eyes to where Evie lay entombed in crystal. "A funeral," he whispered.

The twins stiffened. "What?" they whispered in unison.

Caelum shrugged. "Lytos is right. There is nothing left for us to do. There are no leads on who took her soul, or how. We have tried every spell, brought in every Healer, Soul Searcher, and Death Walker we could find and have nothing to show for it. This is over."

Hex shook his head. "You're giving up?"

Caelum ripped himself from Lytos's grasp and stomped up to Hex, surprised to find they were now eye-to-eye. *When had they grown up so much?* "I'm not giving up. I am admitting defeat. No matter how strong I am, I cannot defeat death."

Pain poured through Hex's body, tainting his heart, scarring his soul, and destroying him to the marrow of his bones. "There has to be a way."

"There isn't! It's too late. I told you to protect her. This never would have happened if you hadn't left her!"

The room released a collective hiss as Caelum glared between Hex and Snip. The boys stood tall, their hurt at the hate-laced words barely perceptible under their practiced stoicism. But Lytos saw. "Caelum, that's enough," he murmured.

160

Caelum shook his head, his eyes bleeding pain and resentment as he fixed them both with a glare. "This is your fault. Both of you. This is on you." With that, he stormed from the room, the door slamming into a silent, stunned room.

"He didn't mean that—" Lytos began.

Hex chuckled, the sound hollow and humorless. "He did. But we appreciate your attempt to excuse him. But he's right. It is our fault."

Hadeon rose from the table and clicked his tongue. "I warned him. I warned all of you. They shouldn't be here. They never should have been—"

Snip snapped his fingers, and the man disappeared. Nalik's jaw dropped, unable to hide his surprise this time. Lytos cleared his throat. "Snip, where did he go?"

"Home," Snip explained as he turned on his heel, slamming the door behind him.

"Hex, he can't just…" Lytos shook his head.

Hex shrugged. "He sent him home. He wasn't welcome anymore. Thank you both for your help. We'll see you at the funeral."

Unlike his brother and father, Hex shut the door softly on his way out.

"Nalik, what do we do?"

Nalik ran a hand through his hair and dropped, exhausted, into an awaiting chair. "I think our only option is to wait and see how this plays out."

"He didn't mean it, right? Surely, he doesn't blame the boys?" Lytos asked. The question hung heavy in the air between them, neither knowing the answer.

Chapter Twenty-Nine

Sleep was elusive. It was always close, weighing down his eyes and limbs, but never quite within reach. But Caelum didn't mind. To sleep was to be vulnerable to his failures as a husband and a father. His sleeping hours were plagued with images of his wife and daughter begging for him to save them while he stood by and did nothing. He would wake with sweat pouring down his body and his heart pounding in his chest. No, he didn't mind the insomnia. He welcomed it.

As another hour ticked by and he remained awake, Caelum counted the night as a loss and climbed from his bed to dress. With a snap of his fingers, a portal opened four steps, he was standing before the tomb that now held both his wife and his daughter.

Moon blossoms shone in the bright light of the full moon, illuminating the beautifully constructed story that Lytos had woven on the tomb's façade not so long ago. Tears stung his eyes and burned his nose. His throat contracted around a sob when the gleaming white chairs for the funeral came into view.

His fingers brushed along the smooth surface as he made his way down the aisle of lilacs. Every step weighed down his heart and dragged silent tears down his face. Caelum swallowed through the thickening in his throat and laid a trembling hand against his daughter's crystalized coffin.

She lay upon a bed of eternal roses, reminding him so much of her mother that he fell to his knees.

"I'm sorry I wasn't there to protect you." he whispered. "I failed as your father and I don't deserve your forgiveness, Evie, but I'm asking you for it." When no response came, Caelum slumped with resignation. His shoulders quaked. He was oblivious to the two lost souls that lingered just inside the shadows.

Hex and Snip stood outside the tomb that housed their mother and now their sister. Their father didn't know they were there, watching and listening to his pleas to the Stars and the string of apologies to his wife and daughter. But that wasn't unusual. Not now. Not since they had carried home Evie's dead body.

Their father, the strongest man they had ever known, had broken before their very eyes. For a week, he had called in spirit specialists, doctors, and even some of the darkest unseelie to find out what had happened in the forest. None of them could find a reason for her sudden death. Only that it was unnatural. Her soul had been forced from her body.

They stood by helplessly as their father slipped further into his grief until it began to rival madness. At night, when he thought they were asleep, he would disappear and scour the Realm for the culprit, only to come back in the morning with defeat hanging over his head.

When the other kings had initially passed blame onto Hex and Snip, they were quickly shot down by their father and their uncles, Lytos and Nalik. But that had quickly changed in the following days. Now the sting of failure was like a festering wound beneath their skin—one that burst under their father's words and spread its guilt-ridden puss through their souls. Their one and only job was to protect their sister, and they had failed.

"We can fix this, Hex."

Hex closed his eyes against the flame of hope. "No, Snip. We can't. It doesn't matter how powerful someone is—no one can defeat death."

Snip shook his head, something unrecognizable glowing in his eyes. "We don't have to defeat death. We just have to go back. If we go back, we can find out what happened and we can stop it."

Hex opened his eyes and searched his brother's. "You're serious."

Snip bobbed his head. "Do you remember the old part of the library? The one covered in the unseelie charms and angel seals?"

"Vaguely…"

"I went there last night. At first, I just wanted to get away. I wanted to find somewhere where no one would stumble across me and ask me how I was doing. But then the seals fell, and the charms faded. I walked through, Hex, and the books inside … the spells they have and the things they promise…"

Hex shook his head. "Snip, no. Those books are locked away for a reason. They wouldn't have put such a heavy guard on them for no reason."

Snip grabbed Hex's shoulders. "They have been sealed away. There but untouchable for generations, and *now* they are reachable! Don't you see? I was *supposed* to find them. We can save Evie!"

"No," Hex whispered, stepping out of his brother's grip.

Snip blinked in disbelief. "What?"

Hex held up his hands and took several steps back. "I said no, Snip."

"We made a promise, Hex. That we would always be there, that we would protect her, and keep her safe. We broke that promise, but we can fix it."

Hex scrubbed his hands over his face and lifted his eyes to the star-littered sky. Their father's soft cries carried on the warm night breeze, dripping grief into his chest like acid into his soul. "I think I know who can help."

Chapter Thirty

Evie's funeral was just as, if not more, beautiful than their mother's had been. Lilacs created a path from the tomb's entrance to where she would forever lie. Lytos had added some of their most fond memories to the beautiful love story he had etched for their mother.

Snip found himself trapped in a sickening déjà vu.

"She's here," Hex said, a sneer tugging at his mouth.

Snip turned to where his brother glared and found Seraphina staring blankly at Evie's casket, her hand trembling as she brought it to hover just above the crystal. "She was her friend, of course she came."

Hex just shook his head as the girl returned to her seat.

Lytos stepped forward with their grief-stricken father in tow. "It's time," he whispered.

Caelum's face crumpled as he stepped toward the podium. His words escaped him as he dragged his eyes from his daughter and into the crowd with their red-rimmed eyes. He shook his head, his mind rebelling at the reality of the task at hand, when, suddenly, Seraphina jerked out of her seat. Caelum's brow twisted in confusion as her indecipherable eyes clashed with his before she fled.

Caelum looked from Seraphina's stunned parents to Lytos. Words once again fled from his mind. Hex and Snip exchanged an angry stare and stepped to their father's side, each placing a hand on his shoulder.

"Evie was light. She was life, and all that was good in this Realm," Hex began.

"Her smile was contagious, and she brought out the best in everyone that she met," Snip continued.

"She never judged or condemned people because of what others thought."

"She was brave and courageous. Loving and strong," Snip added with a sad smile.

"Evie cared. She wanted to make the Realm a better place for everyone, and she did."

"Our sister was the hope this Realm desperately needed. She changed so many lives and our worlds." The brothers' eyes dropped to where their sister lay. Hex cleared his throat as tears stung his nose and watered his eyes. "Evie is, and always will be, our beacon of hope and love."

"She loved us when no one else did." Snip's hand tightened on his father's shoulder, drawing a wince.

"The Stars made a mistake taking her," Hex hissed.

The brothers looked over the gathering with angry eyes. "Pay your respects and leave," Hex ordered.

Lytos sucked in a breath and caught their arms as they stormed from the podium. "I understand your anger, but you can't let it consume you. Feel it and let it go."

Hex jerked his arm away. "They have ten minutes," he whispered.

Lytos frowned. "What do you mean?"

Snip pulled his arm free. "Ten minutes, Lytos. No one wants to see what happens if we are tested."

If the funeral was silent before, it was deathly still now. The twins' callous dismissal had pulled the oxygen from the attendees and replaced it with raw fear. Caelum stepped from the podium, laid his hand upon his daughter's coffin, and murmured a soft prayer.

"Caelum," Lytos interrupted. "You have to talk to them. Before they do something ... rash."

Caelum kissed his fingertips and pressed them against the crystal before turning to his friend. "What they do is not my concern."

Lytos grabbed Caelum's shoulder. "They are your children," he snarled.

Caelum glared at the hand upon his shoulder and shrugged it off. "They are no longer children. You see what they can do. They have secrets no one can unravel, not even me. Their lies have stretched on for years. What would you have me do?"

"Be a father!" Lytos snapped.

Caelum shook his head, his eyes vacant. "You have seven minutes, if my counting is correct."

Lytos watched Caelum walk away with dread twisting in his heart.

"Lytos? Are you alright?"

Turning, Lytos lost himself within the speaker's golden gaze. "Solara."

"Something is brewing. Something dark in those two. If Caelum doesn't step in…" Solara warned.

Lytos sighed and slipped his hand into hers. "I know. But we can do nothing but wait."

Solara rested her cheek against his shoulder and watched Caelum disappear into a portal. "Where do you think he's going?"

"To find answers."

Solara glanced around the dwindling gathering. "Have you told him?"

"Solara," he hissed, eyeing those that watched them with interest. "Now is not the time or place."

"Then find a place and make the time. He needs to know."

"Nalik and I will solve it ourselves. He has enough on his shoulders right now."

Solara jerked her hand from his. "There is never a good time, Lytos. As kings, you will always have a lot on your shoulders. Not sharing information when it is learned is going to be the downfall of this Realm."

"Solara? Lytos? Is everything alright?"

The couple turned with forced smiles toward a worried-looking Marcus. "Yes, fine," Solara lied. "I'll see you later." With a curt tip of her chin, she disappeared into the crowd.

Lytos and Marcus shared a heavy sigh. "She's always been that way," Marcus chuckled.

"Did you think she would get better with age? If we thought she was bad as a child…" Lytos shook his head.

"Come on, I do not wish to find out what those twins have in store if we stay longer."

Lytos glanced at the towering black castle. In all his years of coming to this place, the constant shift and evolution of the stacked square building never ceased to amaze him. "Yes, you're right."

Lytos stepped around Marcus and herded the remaining people through a portal. Marcus lingered, staring up at the shifting castle. It towered high into the sky, a cylindrical telescope wrapped in endless turning gears piercing the clouds. The castle itself resembled a child's haphazardly stacked blocks set upon a revolving table.

Marcus narrowed his eyes at the slowly rotating pieces as lightning slashed and thunder rumbled across the springtime sky.

"Marcus!"

Lytos's summons pulled his attention away from the castle.

"We have to go!"

"Is that … them?" Marcus asked, jerking a finger skyward. The wind lashed his hair against his cheeks.

Lytos's jaw jumped. His only answer was a pointed nod toward their exit. Marcus swallowed his delighted smile and slipped through the static ridden portal.

Chapter Thirty-One

Hex slipped through the library doors, a twinge of satisfaction easing the acid of grief in his stomach. "They are gone."

Snip glance over his shoulder with a malevolent smile. "Did they enjoy the display?"

Hex shrugged. "Is this it?"

Snip stiffened against the chill that threatened to climb up his spine and nodded. "Yes. Strange, isn't it? For years, it would disappear the moment we got close and now … it's just here. Open and ready for the taking."

The twins lingered outside the library's broken enchantments. Hesitation and uncertainty clung to them like a second skin. Hex rolled his shoulders and loosened the tie from around his neck. "This is a terrible idea."

Snip tore his eyes from the musty books and peered at his brother. "It is, but it's the only one we have. Unless, of course, you've thought of something in the last twenty minutes?"

Hex scrubbed a hand over his face. "You know I haven't. We wouldn't be standing here if I had."

"Alright then, let's begin."

Hours turned into days and days into weeks. They only succeeded in filling their minds with useless information that would be stored there forever. Snip shook his head and slammed another book shut. "This isn't working."

Hex snorted and flipped the page of his own book. "Really? I hadn't noticed. Did you know that there is a cell between the Seam and the Membrane where you can trap just about anything?"

Snip rolled his eyes and dropped his head back against his chair. "No, and I don't care. I was so sure. I thought … there had to be something here, otherwise why would there be so many safeguards to keep us out? It doesn't make sense."

Hex dragged his eyes from the fascinating passage and watched his brother spiral. "We've been at it for days. Maybe we just need to take a break—get some rest and come back another time."

Snip shook his head, too lost in his own thoughts to hear Hex's suggestion. "Instead, all we've learned about is hidden cells, lost prophecies, forsaken spells, and outlawed enchantments. None of which can help us." By the end of his tirade, Snip's face twisted with pain. He rubbed at his chest. "We have to find a way, Hex. We have to. I can't do this. It hurts too much."

Hex flinched, knowing the feeling all too well. He tapped his fingers along the smooth, worn tabletop as his mind drifted back to that day.

Snip shifted uncomfortably in his chair. "What?"

"Hmm?"

"You never tap. You hate repetitive noises … unless you have a secret. What is it?"

The tapping picked up, growing more disjointed as Hex gnawed at his lip in indecision. He ran a hand through his hair. "I told you about the day Evie … the day I met Senan in the woods, but I never told you what he said."

Snip rolled his eyes at his brother's slowly drawn-out words. "Stars, Hex! Spit it out before I die, please."

"He said that he wanted something from me."

Snip's brow furrowed in disbelief. "Senan, the all-powerful Eternal, wanted something from *you*?"

Hex nodded.

"What could you possibly do that he can't himself?"

"I have no idea. But … he said that if I did what he wanted, he would give me something in return."

"And what's that?"

"Anything."

Snip frowned and laced his fingers behind his head. "Anything?"

"*Anything*. He made it very clear that anything I wanted he could—and would—provide."

Snip pressed his toes against the ground, balancing his chair on its back legs. "So, you're thinking that he can bring Evie back? I don't know,

174

Hex. Seems pretty unlikely to me. I know Eternals are supposed to be these great all-powerful beings, but to bring someone back from the dead … I think only a reaper can do that. Like *the* Reaper."

Hex dropped his head into his hands. "I suppose you're right."

Snip's chair fell back onto all four legs with a bang. "Do you know where he is?"

"No."

"Do you have any way to contact him?"

"No."

"Do you have a plan on how to find him?"

"No."

Snip groaned and lifted the chair back up. "Stars, Hex. What in Fornax are we supposed to do?"

"Language," Hex snapped. Snip rolled his eyes.

"Am I allowed to weigh in on this?"

Eyes wide, their attention shifted to a low shelf where a large man eating an apple sat. Hex rose gracefully from his seat while his counterpart jerked back in the perfectly balanced two-legged chair, his arms flailing as he tumbled to the ground with a resounding thump.

Senan chuckled as Snip jumped to his feet and straightened his shirt. "Senan, I presume?" Snip asked.

Senan nodded. Mirth glittered in his eyes, making the vines of ebony appear to slither in his silver eyes. "I am."

Snip shifted uneasily. His mind was torn in a battle between his need for his sister and the warning gnawing at his gut. "And you can help us?"

Senan pursed his lips and slid down from the shelf. "Depends."

A growl of frustration rumbled in Snip's throat. "I understand that you have an eternity in front of you and therefore have all the time in the world to draw out this situation, but unlike you, *we* have things to do and people to resurrect. Unless you can help, there's the door."

Senan quirked an amused brow as the stack of books beside him distorted into an impromptu portal. "Flashy," he commended with a chuckle.

Snip ground his teeth.

Hex flinched. "That's enough. Senan, can you help us or not?"

Senan smiled. He enjoyed dangling the twins beneath the weight of his next words. "I can, but you have to do something for me first."

"What?" Snip asked, his breath coming in a rush.

His eyes alight with an unnatural glow, Senan's lips curved into a peculiar smile. "I can help. In fact, we can do it here—now."

Hex narrowed his eyes. "And what do you want?"

Senan slid his attention from one twin to the other. "Just a drop of blood. From each of you."

"A drop of blood? What could you possibly want with that?" asked Snip.

"That's not for you to worry about."

"I think it is. Blood is only used for two things: curses and spells. Which is it?"

Senan dropped his head back in an uproarious laugh. "Don't be ridiculous. What spell or curse can be done with a single drop?" The brothers exchanged a long glance that Senan observed with unveiled interest. "Do you do that often?" he asked. They answered his question with a glare.

Hex twisted his wrist, and a glossy black blade dropped into his outstretched palm. Senan glared at the blade. "Where did you get that?"

Hex smirked but refused to answer. "One drop each and you help us bring Evie back … *tonight*?"

"That's what I said."

Hex wrapped his fist around the hiltless blade and pierced the tip of his finger before handing it to Snip to do the same. The brothers held out their hands as a plump drop formed on the tip of each of their fingers. Hex lifted a brow. "Are you going to let it go to waste?"

Senan withdrew a plain, silver thimble-sized bottle from his tunic and collected first Hex's drop and then Snip's before corking it once more. With a smile, he lifted it to eye level, inspecting the crimson liquid inside. "Alright then, shall we get started?"

Chapter
Thirty-Two

Senan led them through the silent castle until they stood in front of the very doors that haunted their dreams. He pulled the doors wide and stepped into the lightly glowing room while the brothers swallowed around the tightening in their throats and struggled to move their leaden feet forward.

"I don't like this." Snip whispered.

"I don't either, but if being in this room one last time can bring Evie back, it's a small price to pay." Hex swallowed his fear and forced his feet forward. His heart pounded against its cage with every step he took and stalled completely when he saw the table. It had been dragged into the center of the enchanted circle, its pale surface covered with a variety of canisters and jars. Old fear clawed up his throat and smothered his breath. *It's just a room. It's just a room.*

Snip caught his arm. "That's not what I'm talking about!" he hissed.

Hex rolled his eyes. He wasn't a fool. He knew what his brother was worried about. The whole situation was … suspicious. From Senan showing up minutes before they discovered their sister, to asking for a drop of their blood to bring her back, and finally, ending with them in *this* room with the spell and its contents already prepared. Something wasn't right.

"I don't think we should do this," Snip repeated.

"Do you have a better idea?"

"No," Snip said through gritted teeth. "But this doesn't look like a way to bring Evie back. We should find the Reaper and—"

"And what, Snip? Ask him to give her back? The Reaper doesn't care. His job is to manage souls and Evie didn't have hers. There is no guarantee that a Death Walker even brought her over. Father checked with all of them. None of them saw her."

"Then what makes you think Senan's plan is going to work?"

"Because it has to," Hex seethed, jerking his arm free.

Snip ground his teeth and followed Hex to the table where Senan stood, watching them with a strange grin. "Are we ready?" Senan asked.

"No," Snip said.

"Yes," Hex insisted.

Senan lifted a brow at the contradictory answers. "Is there a problem?"

"Yes," Snip answered.

"No," Hex said in a rush.

Hex glared at his counterpart, who stared at Senan, his expression unreadable. "I want to know what this spell is. I don't recognize half of these ingredients and to be in this room … it all seems *wrong*."

Senan lifted his eyes to the room, memories of the past glazing his eyes. "This room is very special. And though every castle of the Seven Kings has a similar one, this is my favorite. They all have ties to the Heart of the Realm, but this room? This room has unique ones."

"What do you mean? What ties?" Snip asked.

"Unlike the others, this room ties directly into the Heart's source. Haven't you ever wondered why your kingdom is the only one with all the seasons and a shifting, ever-changing castle?"

Snip shook his head. "Not really."

Senan pinched the bridge of his nose and released a heavy sigh. "It's fine. Artists go under-appreciated all the time. The point is, with the combination of this spell and this room, we should be able to draw your sister's soul from wherever it was taken and guide it back to her body."

"And it'll work?"

Senan shrugged and pulled the bowl closer. His fingers dipped into and out of the canisters, dropping strange-smelling herbs and powders into the bowl. "I don't see why it wouldn't." Senan paused, a plain jar filled with green liquid poised above the bowl, his face pinched in thought. "Unless…."

Hex stepped forward. "Unless?"

Senan snapped back to the present, blinking rapidly as if clearing a distant thought. He shook his head. "Nothing."

"It certainly seemed like *something*," Snip grumbled. "What is all of this?"

Senan pursed his lips and pointed to the bottles in turn. "Hemlock, fae blood, the good stuff of course."

"Of course," Snip said mockingly, rolling his eyes.

"This is powdered raven's bones, essence of … well, you probably don't want to know." Senan winked and tilted the bottle. Three thick, plump drops landed in the bowl with a loud plop The twin's eyes widened as the bowl began to vibrate.

Hex leaned forward to better examine the misshapen bowl and swallowed thickly. "Is that … is that made from *flesh*?"

Snip jerked in disgust before leaning closer for a better look. The bowl, while seemingly uninteresting, became more gruesome the longer he stared. At first glance, it appeared to be an old, time-discolored wooden bowl. Only wooden bowls didn't have stitching or bulging veins that throbbed with life or the unmistakable presence of tattoos.

"Obviously," Senan snorted.

Snip's eyes widened as he turned to Hex. "Did you catch that, Hex? The bowl is *obviously* made from flesh. This is *definitely* a great idea."

"Your sarcasm is unnecessary," Hex snapped.

"Of course. Because spells with flesh and blood and essence of who-knows-what *always* end well."

Hex whirled on Snip with an icy rage burning in his eyes. "If you don't want to be here, leave."

"Actually, he can't," Senan interjected.

"Excuse me?" the twins asked in unison.

Senan shrugged and lifted a droplet-shaped bottle embedded with a thin green chain. "It's too late. The spell has begun." He tipped the bottle above the bowl, black liquid pouring out.

Chapter Thirty-Three

Smoke twisted and rose from the flesh woven bowl but did not behave as normal smoke would. It didn't rise in a beautiful, swirling manner, stretching high into the air. Instead, it twisted and spread itself wide like fingers before curling into itself like a fist, hovering only inches above the popping blue flame. Snip wrinkled his nose in disgust.

"Hurry!" Senan ordered.

The brothers exchanged one last glance before rounding the table.

Senan pulled a folded slip of paper from his breast pocket and held it out. "Here, say this. Clearly and with all the power you possess."

Hex took the paper and quickly scanned over the words with a worried wrinkle on his brow.

"Where are you going?" asked Snip, as Senan hurried away from the table.

Senan paused and smiled. "The rest is up to you. Don't worry, I translated it into English."

"Senan—"

"You don't have time! The bowl has already begun to change!" Senan said.

With gritted teeth, Hex held out the paper for the both of them to read. "You're not the least bit worried he ran away?"

"Remember: all your strength," Senan added. The brother's bowed their heads and pulled at the endless threads of light from within. Senan watched with unabashed fascination as thin wisps of raw power began to stretch into the surrounding air, bringing a soft shimmer to the air. "Now, hurry," the Eternal insisted.

The brothers lifted their heads, eyes alight with the blinding light of power, their voices reverberating:

> *By air and earth*
> *Fire and water*
> *Darkness and light*
> *What was locked away, let it be freed*
> *By the moon and sun*
> *Sky and sea*
> *Bring it to sight*
> *Bring it this night*
> *As we willed it, so let it be*
> *Darkness released*
> *And now, be bound*

Their last words echoed in the silent chamber. They panted as the last traces of their power receded. "I guess we have a limit," Snip wheezed.

Hex shook his head and fixed Senan with a pointed glare. "What kind of spell was that?"

Senan ignored the question as he spun himself in a circle. "Where is he?"

"Who?" Snip asked.

Senan pulled at the silken strands of his hair in confusion and panic. "Dammit!" he roared.

Hex searched the empty room. "Shouldn't something have happened by now?"

"Should we check the crypt?" Snip asked.

"It didn't work," Senan whispered in disbelief.

Snip's head snapped in Senan's direction. "What are you talking about? You said it would work! We did everything right!"

Senan stalked up to the table, his eyes skimming the recipe and the collection in the bowl. "You must have missed something."

"We missed nothing! We spoke every word. We gave it our all," Hex insisted.

"This was supposed to work," Snip whispered, his eyes locked on the dwindling curl of smoke.

Senan shook his head. "No, you didn't! If you had, he would be here!"

Snip's head snapped up. "He who?"

Senan's eyes rose to meet Snip's.

"What aren't you telling us?" Hex asked.

"This was never going to bring Evie back, was it?" Snip demanded.

Senan's lip curled. Suddenly, the temperature in the room plummeted, and the blood fled from his face, leaving him pale and sweating. Snip watched the vapor puff from his lips as something sickly twisted in his stomach and brought a tremble to his hands.

"We need to leave—now," Senan whispered.

Hex shook his head. "No. You said you would help us. We paid you—now help."

A humorless laugh tumbled from Senan's purple lips. "You don't understand. It's too late. I can't help you."

In the blink of an eye, Snip was in Senan's path, his fists curling into the soft fabric of Senan's shirt and lifting him off his feet. "You lied to us."

Senan flushed with anger, bringing life back into his deathly appearance. "Yes. I did. Are you done?"

Fury pulsed through Snip's heart as he pulled Senan closer. "Not even close." Snip slammed his head forward and the chilly room echoed with the crunch of bone and the Eternal's angry grunt. Senan lifted a hand to his bleeding nose while the other slapped against Snip's chest, sending them hurtling through the air in opposite directions.

Snip flipped head over heels and dug his hand into the frozen stone to stop himself from skidding.

"That was a terrible idea, boy," Senan snarled. The silver of his eyes shivered and shrank until there was nothing but slithering darkness therein. His hand dropped from his nose and the twins watched in morbid fascination as thick, black strands bled from his eyes and sank into the damaged tissue. The loud crack of mending bone resonated in the room.

Snip swallowed the bile rising in his throat Hex stepped close, his body heat warming Snip's chilled body. "We'll be taking our blood back," Hex said.

Senan dropped his head back in boisterous laughter. "Will you?"

"Our deal was broken before it was made."

Senan's dark eyes glittered unnaturally as he pulled the small silver vial from thin air. "Come on then—take it."

At the challenge, glee danced in the twins' eyes. Their lips curved into fanged smiles when a chilling whisper brought a shiver down their spines.

You tried to take what was not yours.

Hex and Snip exchanged a worried glance before turning to find Senan stiff as a board. The Eternal's wide eyes were filled with raw fear.

"What—" Snip began.

You wanted to change the wheels of time.

And bend it to your will.

Several disembodied voices joined together in a building crescendo. A gust of wind washed through the windowless room, flickering the orbs. Senan released a frightened whimper and raced toward the door. The damning click of the lock stopped him in his tracks.

"Senan? What's going on?" Hex asked.

Senan shook his head, his body trembling beneath the knowledge of what was coming. His eyes darted around the room in a frantic search. Hex and Snip watched the Eternal crumble in fear before their eyes and felt their own imminent demise on the horizon.

Senan's body stiffened once more. Figures cloaked in the darkness of shadows surrounded them.

The laws of nature are not yours to play with.

"Wait, please," Senan begged as his doom drew closer.

Your actions have consequences.

Senan cried out as thick, shadowy tentacles wrapped around his body, piercing his flesh with razor-like spikes. He was quickly turned into a sickening display of gasping flesh, blood, and bone.

The twins' mouths dropped open in shock. The oxygen was sucked from their chests, depriving them of life and sending them to their knees. Figures draped in different-colored robes surrounded them like a twisted rainbow from the depths of nightmares. A figure draped entirely in pure white fabric stepped forward.

We all must pay a price for defying nature, White proclaimed.

"Wait," boomed a voice.

Chapter Thirty-Four

The room fell into an expectant silence as the soft footfalls drew closer. The orbs flared with excitement and the spikes withdrew from Senan's body as the newcomer stepped into the circle. A shiver slid down the twins' spines at the sight. Everything about the man was intimidating—from his imposing height and breadth to the striking pale blue eyes set in an emotionless mask, and the terrifying array of weapons he wore. But nothing compared to the menacing waves of power that rolled off him.

Hex frowned, struggling to place the face of the man standing before them. Snip audibly gulped, and Senan's cracked lips curled back in displeasure.

"That can't be," Snip whispered.

"You know who that is?" Hex asked curiously.

Snip nodded. Before he could reply, Senan's snarl severed the silence. "Callen. What do you think you're doing?"

Callen arched a brow, the only movement on his otherwise frozen face. "Is it not obvious? I am here to rescue you. *Again*."

Senan clenched his fists at his sides and took a daring step forward. "I didn't ask for your help. Then or now. You are not wanted here."

The stony-faced man before them cracked a smile as he shoved his hands into his pockets. "Are you sure? It certainly appears as though you are having quite the time. After all, the Iridescent Circle does not show itself for just anyone."

"Iridescent Circle?" Snip whispered. Hex shook his head.

Senan hesitated, his eyes bouncing from the ones draped in shadows to the man he loathed.

"Must you two fight? Even now?" An ivory-skinned woman with raven black hair and large golden eyes stepped around Callen's massive form.

The twins watched with growing intrigue as Senan's posture softened. "Quen. What are you doing here?"

Quen's face fell into sorrow. "Senan, what have you done?"

Senan shook his head and stepped around the robed intruders to take her small, chilly hands in his large, warmer ones. "I'm *saving* us, Quenie. Don't you see? What we did all those years ago was wrong. We need to set things right. Locking them away was wrong."

190

Tears shimmered in the woman's golden eyes, making them shine like the sun. "Senan, whatever he promised you, whatever he said, they were all lies. You know that, don't you? He's using you. Always has and now…" Quen's attention slid to the twins, her face twisting in pain. "Senan, what did you do?"

Senan swiped his tongue over his drying lips and slid his hands up her arms to grip her shoulders. "They don't deserve what we created. You know that, don't you?"

"That isn't your choice to make."

His grip tightened. "No? Then who makes those decisions? Callen?" His laugh was a harsh bark. "The Realm needs a powerful leader, not someone who hides in the depths and *watches*." He sneered.

Callen crossed his arms over his chest. "We are not here to lead, Senan."

Hex watched the exchange with growing fascination while Snip wrapped his hand around his brother's wrist and pulled him slightly back. Hex frowned as he pulled his attention from the story unfolding before them.

We need to go. Now. While we still can. Snip's voice fluttered across his mind. Hex clenched his jaw and slid his eyes over the room. The strange, robed beings stood in a circle around the three Eternals, leaving them completely out of the disastrous situation. Hex dipped his head in agreement and, together, they took a careful step back. When the first went unnoticed, they took another, and then another.

Where are you going?

The twins froze. Not by choice, but by the will of another. The same will that forced one foot in front of the other until they stood back inside the circle.

Snip cleared his throat and forced a smile. "It seems like you guys are dealing with a lot, so we figured you all needed some private time to hash out your issues, and we didn't want to intrude. So, we will just leave you to it."

I am afraid it is too late for that, the one in white said, lifting its hooded head. *It is time.*

The twins swallowed around the gnawing pit in their stomachs. "I'm sorry. Time for what?" Snip asked.

"For your judgement," Callen explained, his eyes still fixed on Senan. "Senan you have been found guilty of treason and sentenced to the Membrane."

Quen's hands flew to cover her mouth as golden tears streamed from her eyes.

"You can't do this," Senan snarled.

"It has already been done."

Senan growled, a deep reverberating sound that rumbled through his chest and echoed in the chamber. His mouth opened, a vicious taunt on the tip of his tongue, when thick, barbed tentacles shot from the shadows to encase his body once more. Agonized screams tore from his throat as the razor spikes tightened and twisted.

Blood streamed from his wounds. His cries faded while his mouth still opened and closed with silent misery. Callen's jaw clenched. Quen cowered at Callen's side, her cries muffled by his bulk. Light emitted from Senan's core. The twins watched in morbid fascination as it stretched the length of his body to consume him entirely. The tentacles encasing him shivered and shrank until there was nothing but a palm-sized stone hovering in the air.

White stepped forward and collected the stone before turning to the twins. *Now, for you.*

Chapter Thirty-Five

Nausea rolled in their stomachs as the fresh memory of Senan's torture flashed through their minds. Their jaws went slack from a blend of shock and raw fear as the robed figures tightened the circle around them like a twisted rainbow. A faint chant began to whisper in the air, ripping the oxygen from their lungs, depriving them of life and forcing them to their knees. The shimmer of white flickered nearby, drawing their attention.

We all must pay a price for defying nature, White proclaimed. The twins watched helplessly as all the figures lifted their hands.

"Just a moment," Callen demanded.

Sweet relief flooded the twins' oxygen-deprived bodies as, one by one, the robed figures dropped their hands. *What is it now?* White hissed.

Callen pulled himself free of Quen's clutches and took several long strides forward. "I have a different sentence. One that I believe is more befitting of their … situation."

And what would that be?

Callen lifted his chin and stared into the depths of its hood. "Senan's sentence was extreme because of his traitorous intent, and while extreme, it fit his crimes. To use the same punishment on these children would be a sentence unbefitting to their own crimes."

White stood in contemplative silence, mulling over Callen's words before finally speaking. *They cannot go unpunished. Whether they knew of Senan's intent or not, they acted against the will of nature.*

"I agree."

What are you proposing, Eternal One?

"Let them become the wards of Time. Let them see what happens when the path is disrupted, and the scales become uneven."

The twins swallowed through parched throats as the circle broke into inaudible whispers. White lifted its hand, silencing the heated debate, and dipped its hood. *As you wish.*

Callen clasped his fist over his chest and slipped into a curt bow. "Thank you." Callen straightened and turned his attention to Hex and Snip. They watched, frozen in place, as silver rolled into his eyes like fog across the sea. "Hexius and Snip of the Sixth Kingdom. You have been found guilty of aiding Senan of the Eternal Ones in defying nature. For your crimes, you have been sentenced to Time."

Hex shook his head, his brow furrowing in incomprehension. Snip opened his mouth to speak when Callen shifted abruptly. The space between them disappeared in an instant. His enormous hands pressed firmly against their chests. The twins hissed in a breath, flinching back to prepare for the onslaught of pain. But the pain did not immediately come. Just as relief began to trickle into their souls, it all changed.

Icy heat, both chilling and burning, seeped from Callen's hands, and poured into their chests, spreading out and filling them from the tips of their toes to the ends of their hair. Their vision blurred and darkened as inexplicable pain claimed the marrow of their bones and the life from their souls. Silent screams parted their mouths as their agony intensified, leaving them writhing on the cobbled ground.

They knew nothing outside of their pain. Their bodies and minds became a prison as fire and acid raced through their veins. Their minds raged against their confines as their souls screamed for reprieve.

As they reached the precipice of death, their hands outstretched in greeting, life's breath rushed into their lungs and flooded their cells, bringing a needle-like sensation to their limbs. Callen stepped into their field of vision and knelt to meet their eyes with pity and sorrow in his own.

"I did not have the power to stop what was coming but know that what I have done saved your lives. Even if in the coming days it does not seem that way."

"What did you do?" Snip gasped.

Callen's eyes flickered with regret. "For attempting to tamper with time, you have become the prisoners of Time itself."

Hex shook his head. "What does that mean?"

Callen stood and looked down at them. "Time is your warden. Your end will not come without its consent. For your treasonous acts against the scales, neither of you will see the end of your days. Soon, Time will share its inevitable burden and you both shall forever exist as its observer and keeper."

Snip rose to his feet in shock as wave after wave of raw power filled his cells. "I feel invincible," he whispered, staring at his trembling hands.

Hex snorted, his chest heaving with unsteady, forceful breaths. "Feeling and being are two very different things." He sat back against his heels. Icy teardrops trailed from the corners of his eyes. With a frown, he swiped at his cheeks and blanched when they came away bloody. "Snip," he whispered.

Snip turned. His eyes widened at the sight of his kneeling brother. Hex's already dark hair had darkened into the color of a moonless night, while his eyes were as red as freshly spilled blood.

Hex frowned. "Snip? What's—?" His words broke off as he motioned to his brother's chest. Snip's eyes fell to the burnt portion of his left side and hissed a breath between his teeth. His skin was sunken and black, as if someone had branded him with a twisted coil of metal. Snip lifted his fingers and brushed it along his red-lined skin. When he looked up at Hex, he realized his twin's skin was also marred, albeit on his right side.

Lost in their own confusion, the brothers were completely oblivious to the disappearance of the rainbow-cloaked figures, until a chilling whisper brought them back to the moment. *This is the last time that I can help you,* White said.

Callen dipped his head in appreciation. "Yes. Thank you."

White lifted its hand, revealing the gemstone that now contained Senan floating above its palm. *I assume you will want to take this with you?*

Callen jerked his head in the affirmative.

The last time, White reminded him, dropping the gem into Callen's hand and disappearing before it could settle upon his palm.

"What in Fornax did you do?!" Snip raged.

"What is this?" Hex asked, poking the marred flesh on his chest.

Callen's jaw ticked as he closed his fist over the warm gem. He stared at his fist for several moments before forcing his attention back to the brothers. "The mark of Time. Remember who you are in the coming days. Do not let the power twist your mind."

The brothers exchanged a confused glance, ready to voice a hundred questions, but before they could utter a single one, Callen and Quen disappeared into the ground.

CHAPTER THIRTY-SIX

One week later

It was dark, but somehow, Snip could see into the empty expanse. Panic thrummed through his veins. "No," he whispered. "Not again."

As the plea left his lips, faces flickered in the darkness. Each with hundreds of copies, all in different states of emotion and phases of life. Mangled corpses littered the floor, leaving a dizzying array of blood and gore splashed across the Empty.

Slowly, the bodies moved, drifting closer to others as scenes began to unfold and play out at a dizzying speed. Snip's stomach rolled and bile climbed his throat as he dropped to one knee. A flash of red caught his eye and brought him to his feet. He hadn't seen it before, and change meant something was coming.

"Wait! Please!" he begged, racing after the red slip. His steps faltered. A girl? Snip shook his head and ran faster, his fingers brushing against the soft fabric of her shirt.

"Don't," snapped a voice.

Distracted, Snip stumbled, and the girl disappeared from sight. A frustrated groan passed his lips as he turned to find the culprit.

Snip jerked upright in his bed, his body dripping with sweat. A roar passed his lips as he tossed the blanket aside and paced the cold stone floor. His dream played on repeat, the confusing images flashing before his eyes, distorting his surroundings. He could still see the corpses crawling across his bedsheets, reaching out of his dresser drawers.

Tugging at the silken strands of his hair, another roar left his lips. He wanted to silence the voices—to stop the endless images that ran through his mind. Even when awake, the past and present collided in his mind's eye, infinite possibilities unraveling. Desperation crested the horizon of his soul as madness clawed its way to freedom. He was losing his grip on reality, unable to differentiate his thoughts from those of something *other* lingering inside. The present and the potential future had become muddled.

His fingers twisted into the roots of his hair and pulled. The burn of pain offered him a moment of reprieve before the chatter began once more. Frustrated, he swiped the contents of his desk to the floor.

"Having issues?"

Snip stiffened and turned to glare at his brother, who leaned against the doorframe. He was different now. But they both were. Before the blunder of a ceremony, they had been perfect copies. Now, the only thing they shared was the sharpness of their cheeks and onyx hair. Blood had crept into Hex's grey eyes, staining them with an eerie vibrancy. Conversely, Snip had been consumed by the depths of his sins, leaving his eyes as black as his forsaken soul. In the days since their "punishment," they had grown wary of one another. The voices they were forced to live with and the sights they were forced to see caused paranoia to bubble up to the surface.

"Hex, how nice of you to check in."

Hex shoved from the door frame, invading Snip's personal sanctum. "Yes, well, I figured we should get things worked out now before you completely lose your mind."

Snip ground his teeth at the implication and felt something shift inside. The voices agreed with him. "I'm not going to lose my mind, Hex. Whether or not you believe it, I'm stronger than I look."

Hex fixed his blood red stare on his brother. "Are you? I know you saw me there."

Snip narrowed his eyes.

"I've been watching you over the last week, as you have me. The dreams are growing in frequency, and you are losing your grip on reality. I can tell that you're an inch away from giving in."

"You don't know what you're talking about."

Hex chuckled and tapped a finger beside his eye. "It shows here. That dark little gaze of yours slithers when you let them get too close."

"And yours gets bloody. What's the point?"

"We can't give in."

"I won't."

"We don't know what the council did to us."
"Aside from the obvious?" Snip quipped.

"I'm trying to help you!"

"Who said I wanted your help?"

"Dammit, Snip! This isn't a game. Do you understand what can happen if you let go? If either of us let them take control?"

Snip smirked. "No, do you?"

Hex gritted his teeth and, with a shake of his head, stormed from the room.

One Month Later

Their minds twisted, leaving them with fewer moments of clarity; warped versions of the truth. Their energies were volatile and unstable, manifesting as destructive storms, floods, and suspicious glares over the table. Callen's warning rang in their ears day after day. *Remember who you are… Do not let the power twist your mind.* But had it really happened? Or was it just another possibility?

Snip glared out the large library windows, watching as the smiling townspeople strolled through the spring, while his world crumbled with every day the sun dared to rise. His teeth ground together. With a burst of anger, he slammed his hand against the glass, splintering it beneath his palm. Black clouds rolled into view, plump droplets raining down upon the unsuspecting citizens, making them scatter to seek shelter. A cruel smile crested his lips as Hex strode into the room, forcefully slamming the doors against the wall, cracking the frames and splintering the crown molding. Amused, Snip arched a brow. "Brother, how nice to see you."

"I know what you did."

Snip chuckled. "Do you now? And what would that be?"

"We made a deal. Summer and fall are *mine*. You broke the agreement."

Thick lines webbed out from Snip's eyes, bulging the sides of his face. "Excuse me?"

"Your people are breeching my property."

Snip scoffed. "Your property? I thought we were running this kingdom together … at least until Father enters the world again."

The ground began to quake as the twins' conflicting power struggled to overtake the other. "We had a deal."

"What deal?" Snip growled. Books clattered to the floor as the quakes shook the carefully lined shelves. "We never made a deal."

"Liar," Hex hissed. "Shall we finish this once and for all?"

Snip pursed his lips and clicked his teeth. "What do you have in mind?"

Hex smiled and turned toward the door. "Come along."

Snip watched his brother slip through the doorway without so much as a backward glance. With pursed lips and hands shoved into his pockets, he let his curiosity win and followed.

The halls were silent, empty, and cold. The storm raging outside rattled the windows.

Hex flicked his wrist, opening the large entryway doors with a deafening creak to reveal the dry courtyard. Snip's brow furrowed. The thunderous storm slammed against something high in the sky, sheltering the courtyard.

"A barrier," he mumbled.

"This isn't your first tantrum, brother." Hex chuckled.

Snip stomped after Hex. "What are we doing here?" he growled.

"Do you know what this spot is?" Hex asked, pointing to the engraved star between them in the courtyard's center.

"It's the convergence of the seasons. What of it?"

"There is a very special board just beneath its surface. A board that has the power to alter fate." Hex bent to lay his hand atop the engraving.

"Alter fate, you say. How so?"

Hex stood and stepped back as the center of the star separated, rose, and folded itself into a large table with a hollow center. Hex motioned for Snip to sit in one of the rising chairs and settled into the other. "It's quite simple, really. It takes control of the players and uses their souls as collateral."

As he spoke, a board made of marble, encased, and embedded with twisted metal scrollwork, rose and claimed the table's center. Black and red pieces sprang up from the checkered pattern.

"Have you forgotten, brother? Our souls are no longer ours to control," Snip snickered.

"Shall we play and find out?"

Snip's smile darkened. "Why don't you expand the barrier a bit?"

"What are you talking about?"

"Oh come now, Hex. You don't think I missed you covering the Realm in a barrier this morning, do you?"

Hex laid his head against the back of his chair. "Then you will play?"

Snip nodded as he settled into his chair.

Hex snapped his fingers. "Done."

Snip smirked as he reached for a robe-draped pawn. "And the winner gets what?" he asked, moving it forward. The ground rumbled beneath a stampede of feet.

Hex lifted his knight and slammed it down. The air echoed with the scraping of metal and static of electricity. "Whatever is left."

Snip lifted another robed pawn and dropped it against the last. "Sounds fair."

Chapter
Thirty-Seven

Battle cries shattered the morning's peace. Explosions rattled the windows and the light of magical warfare flashed upon the horizon. The six Kings sat in horrified silence. Dorrin and Casimir stared out the large windows with dark excitement glittering in their eyes. Lytos and Hadeon stared at Caelum, who did nothing to hide his disinterest.

The silence between the men stretched on. Their impatience took the form of tapping fingers, bouncing legs, and annoyed sighs. Caelum hadn't wanted this meeting and was only here because Lytos had begged him to hear the other kings out. He was already regretting the decision.

Another round of tortuous cries fluttered through the windows. Lytos flinched at the palpable pain that tinged the air. Sadness pulled down his brow as he looked, once again, at Caelum. His friend didn't care. The state of the kingdom no longer mattered to Caelum. That much was clear in his posture. Instead of keeping with formalities, Caelum leaned back in his chair with an ankle crossed over his knee and his chin resting upon his fist.

Lytos released a heavy sigh. "Caelum—"

Hadeon slammed his fist against the table, rattling their glasses. "I told you their birth was an omen of terrible things to come! But you didn't want to listen and now look at the state of things."

Caelum lifted his empty eyes, his tone apathetic. "What goes on in my kingdom is none of your concern."

"It doesn't seem to be yours, either. The Seven Kings' Bond—"

"The Seven Kings' Bond was put into place to stop quarreling *between* kingdoms. It has nothing to do with what goes on within one."

Hadeon's nostrils flared in anger. Seeing that he was getting nowhere with Caelum, he turned his attention to Lytos. "Does this not concern you? Watching your best friend fall into the pits of despair and leaving his spawn to incite a civil war?!"

Caelum's eyes darkened. The first display of any emotion Lytos had seen in the months since his daughter's death. "I would watch what you say about my *spawn*."

"Caelum," Lytos began. "As much as it sickens me to say it: Hadeon is right. Hex and Snip have been overtaken by their grief. Something has …

changed inside of them. They are no longer the children that you raised. They are using the Board of Fate. They are condemning your citizens to death."

"That may be, but we all change when forced into the bowels of what life has to offer. Grief changes you in unrecognizable ways. I am no longer the man you knew." Caelum rose from his chair and strode to the door. "You can all see yourselves out."

"Caelum!"

Caelum paused with his hand on the doorknob. "What is it, Lytos?"

"I know losing your daughter was hard, that it is tearing you apart, but to let Hex and Snip run wild like this…" Lytos faltered as he struggled to find the words that would bring Caelum from his sorrow. "They blame themselves."

"Perhaps they should." Caelum snarled, whirling to face the other kings. His rage contorted his face.

Lytos jerked back as if he had been struck. "You don't mean that, Caelum. Tell me you don't believe those boys are at fault for what happened to Evelyn."

"They had *one job*."

"Crixus, Caelum! Do you hear yourself? How often did Evie walk through those woods alone? Once a week? Twice? You have let your grief make you bitter and have placed the blame where it doesn't belong."

"They left her alone, to fend for herself."

Lytos scoffed. "Oh please, she wasn't a dainty flower."

"Stars knows who or what stumbled upon her and took her life. Her *soul* was gone, Lytos. Her body was cast aside. Who does that?" Nalik asked.

Lytos glared at the smirking trio. "I know of a few people."

Hadeon dropped his head back in outrageous laughter. "Trying to throw the blame, Lytos? How very childish of you."

"Did you think we didn't know of your soul warping, Hadeon? Of the experiments you do while hidden in the deepest, darkest hole you can find?"

Hadeon's smile fell away and Casimir and Dorrin shifted slightly in their seats. "I do not know what you're talking about. We aren't here to talk about rumors, we are here to talk about the civil war that Caelum has let his sons begin."

"Since when does anything in my kingdom concern you?"

"Since the bombs and spells can be seen from my windows! Your lands border mine. My people are at risk if your battles spread any further."

"Don't worry, that won't happen. The boys have placed several protective barriers around the kingdom. No one comes in without permission and no one leaves without being cast out," Caelum replied with a smirk.

Hadeon's eyes flared with curiosity. "They did *what*? How?"

Caelum tsked. "Now, now, Hadeon, what would give you the impression that I would ever tell you that?"

Hadeon flushed with loathing. "I wasn't aware that we kept secrets from each other."

Caelum snorted. "Yes, *this* is the only secret being kept."

"What's that supposed to mean?" Dorrin asked.

"The bond prevents us from waging war on a physical front. But that hasn't stopped you three from conducting your twisted experiments and setting them free upon the Realm. Monsters without souls or masters. We have been investigating them for a while now, haven't we, Lytos?"

Lytos glowered at Caelum. Their investigation had been kept quiet for a reason. If the trio didn't know someone was watching, they were bound to make a mistake that would lead to their exile. Dorrin, Casimir, and Hadeon exchanged a nervous expression before narrowing their eyes at Lytos.

The castle shook with another explosion. This time, the blast was much too close for anyone's comfort. Caelum looked out the cracked window with indifference. Everyone else rose to their feet.

"We are getting off topic," said Lytos. "We need you to stop your sons before it's too late."

"I think it's time for you all to leave."

"Y-y-you must be joking," Hadeon sputtered.

"You have five minutes, and then I set my *spawn* on you."

Lytos shook his head. "What in Fornax has happened to you?"

Caelum slammed his palm against the door, rattling it on its hinges. "What's happened to me? I had my wife and daughter ripped away. *That's* what happened to me. Four minutes."

"Caelum, please. If you don't stop them, your kingdom will fall."

"Then it will fall."

Chapter Thirty-Eight

Two Years Later

Snip seethed. Darkness bled into the bulbous veins around his eyes. "It stole our control. Knocked us out of balance."

Hex chuckled and slid his castle across the board. "Who are you trying to fool? The mark did nothing we haven't asked it to. We have spent our lives searching for a reason—for the slightest reason—to let ourselves taste the freedom of no restraint. Our warden simply served it up to us. Check."

Snip's eyes fell to the board. He thought back through the years and settled upon the moment when emotion overran logic and impulse had taken over. "We were children." He slid his own castle across the board to defend his king.

Hex shook his head and made his own castle retreat. "Have you not realized what our game has done yet, brother?"

Snip lifted his castle and froze. His head jerked up as his clear eyes swept over the kingdom. The seasons joined together around them. Spring, once vibrant and lively, was a burnt wasteland that left winter stained in a sinful, bloody pattern. Bile climbed his throat when he continued his inspection. Autumn smoldered with large craters, denting the earth and severing trees. But summer … summer turned his stomach as the wind pulled its stench into his nostrils.

His hand shook as he swallowed against the blooming nausea. Hex chuckled darkly. "Don't worry. The survivors are long gone. They ran. When you had your … *moment* and our game paused, their minds were freed from our hold. I'm sure they are off telling the tales of the crazed brothers and their devastating actions. I think we have become infamous, brother."

Snip shook his head and slammed his piece down, rattling the board. "I don't understand."

Hex shifted in his chair and rested his chin on his fist. With a sigh, he slid the next piece. "I didn't think you did. You see, this board of ours isn't an ordinary board. Nor are its pieces or this platform. The combination of its curse and our newfound … abilities have altered their true purpose."

Snip's jaw ticked. "Check. You knew?"

Hex arched a brow as he slid his bishop. "Of course. How else were we going to settle this dispute of ours?"

Snip gritted his teeth as he shifted his castle. "All of this so you could rule over this broken kingdom?" he hissed.

"Of course not. This was all to see how far we would go."

Snip's eyes shifted back to the rot that had become of summer. Steam rose from bloated corpses while others were being picked over by giant vultures and snarling wolven shifters. Tremors rippled down his arms as he struggled to comprehend his morbid fascination at the effects of a simple game. He was sickened by his role in it.

Hex watched his brother struggle with a smile. "Are you going to play?"

Snip blinked, examining the remaining four pieces with a furrowed brow. "This game will never have a winner."

Hex arched a brow. "Are you forfeiting?"

Snip's eyes darkened once more. "Never," he snarled. "We are at a draw. Neither willing to concede."

Hex sighed. "Yes, I suppose you are right. Shall we begin again?"

"NO," boomed a voice. "You are done. I will not let this continue."

Hex and Snip straightened in their chairs, neither willing to take their eyes off the board—or each other. After a wary standoff, they turned toward the man who dared command them.

Their father rested a hand for support against one of the remaining pillars, looking more tired than either could remember.

"Father," Hex said coldly. "How lovely to see you. It's been what? One, two years now?"

"What are you doing here? Have you finally dragged yourself from the pits of your own despair to remember us?" Snip asked.

Caelum's jaw clenched, glaring at the opulent setup lingering in the air between his sons. "This has gone on long enough. I have let you wage your war and take out your anger for each other on this kingdom for far too long. We have each lost ourselves in grief. It is time to dig ourselves back out of the pits we have made."

Snip clenched his fists and rose, stalking to the edge of the enchanted circle. "The pits *we* made? You abandoned us! You left us alone, while you wallowed. We tried to bring her back, we tried to fix it, knowing you blamed us! This is your fault!"

"Snip," Hex warned.

Snip turned with a withering glare, his eyes following his brother's gaze to the edge of the circle. If he took another step, he would have left the circle and cemented his fate.

Caelum frowned as he took in the full scene. "What have you done?"

"It's the Board of Fate. The board that control the souls. Don't you recognize it, old man?" Snip taunted. "It's the soul board."

Caelum's eyes flared. "You bet your lives in a chess match?"

Hex smirked. "Have you forgotten, *Father?* We have no souls and therefore have nothing to wager."

Caelum frowned, then paled as understanding fell upon his shoulders. "You used the people in the kingdom. Why?"

Snip clapped his hands. "Congratulations. You figured it out. Several years too late. Even so, good job."

"Why would you do that?! You stole their minds and condemned their souls for an eternity!"

Hex shrugged and unfolded himself from his chair. "Isn't it obvious? We needed to decide who would run the kingdom since you were … indisposed."

Caelum arched a brow. His eyes roamed over the once thriving, vibrant kingdom, which he and his wife had built. The unique placement of the kingdom meant that all four seasons rotated throughout the kingdom in waves. Now it lay in ruins.

The seasons had been replaced with the stages of war. Blood had chased away the gleam of winter. The flowers of spring wilted beneath the polluted, ominous air. Summer was tainted by the smell of decay. Autumn held nothing—the trees' branches were bare and the bushes devoid of the berries that Evelyn had once baked into pies. The string of homes that had held its citizens had long sensed emptied, leaving nothing but the ghost of happiness behind.

His prosperous kingdom had fallen, just as Lytos had predicted, and he had done nothing to stop it.

Caelum descended the stairs with heavy steps. His lip curled when the breeze brought with it the stench of death. "You are both done. I am here to put an end to this nonsense."

Hex laughed. He couldn't help it. The thought that his father would do anything to either of them—that he would even think of them—was preposterous.

Caelum's jaw twitched at the obvious display of disrespect. "Is something amusing to you, son?"

Hex's smile gleamed in the dying light. "Am I your son now?"

Caelum frowned and looked between the pair. They had changed. They were taller, broader, and older. Their faces no longer matched as perfectly as they had in childhood. The rich darkness of their hair and sharpness of their cheeks remained mirrored, while nearly everything else had changed.

Snip's once light grey eyes were empty onyx pits. The laughter they had once held had dimmed in the wake of life's cruelty. His hair was erratically spiked around his head and two days' worth of beard lined his jaw.

But it wasn't the changes in Snip that frightened him the most. It was Hex—sweet, intelligent, loving Hex. His pale eyes that had once shone with curiosity and the thirst for knowledge were filled with something darker and stained blood red. There was no warmth in his gaze, only loathing.

"What have you two done?"

They exchanged a glance, causing Caelum's heart to squeeze painfully in his chest. The simple gesture sent them back to the years of their childhood. "A little late to be asking that, isn't it?" asked Snip.

"What in Fornax has gotten into you?!" Caelum demanded.

"Time. All of it. The past, present, and future. It has the tendency to drive one mad when you can see it all *right here*." Hex tapped the side of his head.

Chapter Thirty-Nine

Caelum felt his failure in the marrow of his bones. His neglect stared him in the face, almost suffocating in its intensity. "This is over. It is time to move on and rebuild," he insisted.

Hex smirked at the bleached version of his father. "You can't change what has been done or stop what is coming."

"I may not be able to change the past, but I can stop you."

Snip snorted at the thought. "You can stop us? In what world?"

Caelum's jaw clenched, his sad eyes falling on Hex. "I don't have to stop both of you. Only one."

Snip frowned as Caelum sprang into motion. The movements were so precise, so quick, that Snip could barely follow. In a blur of a moment, Snip was cast from the enchanted circle as Caelum took his place. Hex's eyes drifted to Snip's in a single, silent clash as their father's hand rose between them.

"I'm sorry," Caelum whispered.

Hex smirked as he watched his father's hand rise and consume him with light.

Fifteen Minutes Earlier

Clarity penetrated Hex's brain like the sun parting the clouds after a week of fog. Destruction fluttered at the edges of his vision and twisted his stomach. He knew what he had done. What Snip had done. He hadn't been possessed or overtaken. The decisions he had made were ones that had always lingered in the back of his mind. But he hadn't meant to act on them. Or had he?

Hex swallowed around the lump of remorse lodged in his throat and glanced up at his brother. Snip's brow was furrowed in concentration as he carefully analyzed the remaining four pieces on the board. The madness was faint in his brother's eyes, overwhelmed by his competitive spirit.

The wind shifted, and the smell of burned flesh tickled his nose. The kingdom was quiet, empty of chirping birds and buzzing bees. The chatter of its citizens was long gone, and yet, Hex felt nothing regarding their loss. Only the loss of the beauty that had been his home affected him.

Hex shifted against the uncomfortable slithering within his bones and decided. A quick glance revealed Snip's concentration hadn't waned and Hex closed his eyes. It was a strange feeling; one he wasn't sure he would ever get used to. Stripping his essence from his body was an unusual mix of pain and freedom. While his body remained stationary within the binding circle, his mind flew like a lightning bolt through the sky.

He didn't have to search. He knew where his father would be, and disgust shook his body to find himself right. Caelum sat in the dark, leaning against the foot of Evie's pink, ruffle-covered bed. He brushed his fingers against the enchanted images twisting before his eyes. This was a new memory. A custom one that his father had created in the depths of his grief. Hex watched his mother and sister settle themselves into their favorite part of the garden and allowed himself to indulge in his mother's musical voice before clearing his throat.

His father barely glanced at him before his eyes fell back to the moving image. "What do you want?"

"I'm here to ask for your help."

Caelum snorted, his lips twisting in a half-smile. "What for?"

Enraged, Hex kicked at his father's foot. His incorporeal foot slipped through his father's solid one.

Caelum's brow rose as gooseflesh prickled upon his skin. With narrowed eyes, he glared at his son. "You're not actually here. How?"

"Astral projection, Father. A skill that every traveler has if only they practice."

"Mmm. Is there no end to your abilities?"

Hex knew the question was rhetorical and biting but choose to answer anyway. "Not yet. Which brings me to the matter at hand. You need to send me away."

Caelum scoffed. "Do I? How do you propose I do that?"

"With this." Hex snapped his fingers and an old, tattered slip of paper fluttered into his father's lap.

"What is it?"

"A containment spell."

Caelum arched a curious brow. "And it will work?"

Hex pursed his lips. "No. It won't keep me in, but it will dampen my strength and hide me from this world. At least for a little while."

"Why would you do that?"

"Because my brother and I have become the wards of time and when we are together… well, you've seen what happens. Our power brings out the worst in each other. Most of the time, we're not in control. We need time apart to come to terms with what has happened and learn to control ourselves."

"If you knew, why didn't you leave before you destroyed my kingdom?"

"If you cared, why didn't you stop it!" Hex seethed, then forced himself to take a deep breath. "I don't have much time. You have ten minutes to decide, and then it is out of my hands."

"Why are you doing this?"

"Because I promised to always protect my brother."

Caelum glared at his eldest. "Like you did your sister?"

"Yes. I gave everything for her. One day, when you see her and mother again, perhaps you will see that. Ten minutes."

Caelum watched his son disperse into a thousand shards.

Snip lifted an arm to shield his face as the searing light consumed everything in its path. His body itched as the light poured over his skin. A tortured groan vibrated in Caelum's chest as his light devoured his son. As the remnants of Hex faded away, Caelum dropped his trembling hand and staggered back.

Snip lowered his arm and blinked the spots from his vision. His breath caught in his throat as he found a deep cavern where his brother once stood. "What happened?! Where is he? What did you do to him?!"

Caelum shook his head. "This had to end."

Snip bared his elongating teeth and wrapped his fists into his father's shirt. "Where. Is. He?"

"Gone. Locked away far from here."

Snip shoved Caelum from his grasp and ran his hand through his hair. A howl tore its way free of his chest.

"I couldn't let you two tear each other apart. I am your father—"

"No!" Snip roared. "You don't get to be a father now. When you got the chance, you did the same as everyone else. You condemned us."

"And that was my mistake. But Snip, this can't go on. The Realm—"

Caelum's eyes fluttered in confusion, his legs buckling beneath him, dropping him to his knees. Warmth, thick and sticky, seeped into his clothing as pain lanced through his body.

Snip watched his father fall, an echo of emotion flickering across his face. "Father?"

Caelum looked up with defeat and remorse in his eyes. "I'm too late. The Realm has fallen."

Snip stiffened. "What?"

Caelum lifted his hand, fresh blood dripping from his fingertips. "Lytos has severed the Seven Kings' Bond."

Snip's head swam at his father's words. "But that means…"

Caelum forced a smile through the building of indescribable pain. "Stay strong. Never give in, Snip. Be here for the Realms."

Snip dropped to his father's side just as he took a final shuddering breath and shut his eyes for the last time. "Realms? What are you talking about? Father!"

The earth trembled beneath his feet, crying out in agony as something nefarious wove its deadly web. Something unseen slapped at the barrier he and Hex had erected before their game—testing it, probing for a weakness. Each hit was more deafening than the last until suddenly, an all-consuming silence descended. Snip panted. A frown lined his face as, for a moment, everything seemed to return to normal.

Then the cruel reality of the severed bond descended. The kingdom remained, in all its brutal destruction. But that was all that survived. The edge of the barrier saving him from the endless sea of nothing surrounded the destroyed paradise. Snip stumbled to the edge and watched with growing panic as the earth hovered above nothingness. He was alone. Totally, completely, utterly, alone.

Chapter Forty

Several Forgotten Years Later

He had been wandering the darkness for ages, following a barely lined path toward his goal. The map he had been given was his only source of light, and even that was barely legible beneath the oppressive darkness.

He would be remiss if he didn't acknowledge his own fear that he had been sent on a fool's errand. After all, he was just another man standing on a low rung in the ladder of power. But this was his chance to prove himself. His chance to change the trajectory of his life.

After another hour roaming the darkness, his doubts grew to near immeasurable heights. The defeated sigh that left him echoed like a scream in the dead of night. He flinched as the sound came back to grate upon his ears.

A snap sounded, followed by a radiant ball of light.

The man blinked several times to dispel the stars that danced before his eyes while his mind struggled to comprehend what he was seeing. Excitement spurred his steps and drew him closer, a smile curving his lips when the prize he had sought revealed itself.

A man sat on the floor with his head tipped back, his smoldering red eyes shimmering in the soft light he held between his fingers. The man lifted his chin and swallowed through his fear as he stepped closer. Runes of every shade and language pulsed to life in thick strands. The man's narrowed at the sound of a hoarse chuckle.

"You didn't think this was a *normal* prison, did you?"

The haggard man's dark hair blended almost seamlessly into the surrounding darkness. While his pale skin appeared to be lit by an ethereal glow.

The man cleared his throat. "I am here to offer you a deal." he said, receiving a snort in return. "You are Hexius?"

Something slithered within Hex's cherry red gaze. "I am."

The man nodded. "My employer would like to offer you a deal."

"Is that so?" he asked.

"Yes," the man said with a smile.

In an instant, Hex was at the magical bars, the movement so quick and unexpected that the man reeled backward, his heart thudding in his chest. Hex chuckled and moved back to his spot on the floor. "And what deal would that be?"

The man cleared his throat, his voice taking on a practiced tone. "You have been sentenced to a life between the in-between. Your choice is simple. Stay here, in this paradox between heaven and hell, or…"

Hex lifted his head with fire blazing in his hungry red gaze. "Or?"

"Or you agree to work with us, and I set you free."

"I think there has been a misunderstanding."

The man's brow furrowed. "Has there? Because from where I stand, you are trapped within a prison that you yourself created, sentenced to an eternity of imprisonment by your own reflection."

This time, Hex made a show of unfolding his body and rising to his feet. His steps were calculated as he made his way to the invisible lining of his cell and stopped. A humorless smile curved his lips as he spoke. "A creator can never truly be trapped within his own creation."

The stranger paled as Hex took another step forward, freeing himself of his own confines. He shook his head. "I don't understand."

"And that is why you don't stand a chance against me. I let my brother believe he had trapped me here for his own peace of mind, to repay a debt he had no business paying." Hex looked about the depths of light and dark that severed the room in half before placing his attention back on the stranger. "I have been here for your protection. For the protection of everyone that has been trying to fix the wrongs that I allowed to transpire."

The stranger forced himself to remain standing when all he wanted to do was crumble beneath the weight that had sucked the oxygen from his lungs.

Hex clasped his hands behind his back and leisurely circled the man. "This prison wasn't built to keep me inside; it was built to keep everyone else out. To shield me from the outside world so that no one would ever find me. Though I must admit, I am curious. How did you find me?"

The stranger forced himself to stand tall beneath Hex's dense scrutiny. "I was given a map and strict orders to follow."

Hex stopped in front of the man, his lips pursed in thought. His imprisoned mind slowly came back to life to dissect his memories. "And the person behind these orders?"

The man swallowed thickly; the action caused the protruding knot in his throat to bob. "I am not at liberty to say."

Hex smiled and draped his power around him like a cloak. The man breathed in several deep, grateful breaths. Hex watched him in amusement before lifting his leg and striking it against the inside of the stranger's. A sickening pop echoed in the dense, silent room. As the man fell to the ground, Hex twisted his hand in the fabric of his shirt and dragged him to eye level. The man whimpered beneath the full blaze of Hex's glowing red gaze.

"Now then, why don't you just show me what I've missed these past few years?"

Whimpers tumbled from the man's lips as his pain-filled eyes glazed over. He shook his head. "Please, you don't understand. He will kill me."

Hex smiled. "Why are you frightened of a man that is not here when a monster holds you in his clutches?" He lifted a glowing hand.

"Please no," the man begged.

"Don't worry, it'll be over soon."

The instant contact was made, pain seared through the man's mind as memories were forced to play out before his eyes. A never-ending scream tore from his lungs. The shrill, raw sound echoed into the depths of the darkened abyss.

Hex withdrew his hand as the man curled into himself, sobbing.

"So, the Realms have fallen, and little brother is playing savior with Averie." Hex pursed his lips at the sight before snapping his fingers. The air shifted, pulled into a swirling distortion. "I'll leave this open for five minutes. I'm assuming you can pull yourself together by then."

"Wait!" the man croaked. "My boss wants to talk to you."

Hex shook his head. "Sorry, but I have other plans."

The man watched Hex step through the portal, helpless to stop him under the wave of pain that threaded through his body. Dropping his head to the cool ground, he slammed his fist against the floor. Suddenly, the temperature plummeted. His breath came out in quick white puffs.

"You failed," a grating voice said.

The man shook his head. "No, I tried."

"And failed."

Light erupted, washing away the shadows for a single moment before darkness consumed the place that had once been Hex's cage. The air filled with the acrid smell of burnt flesh, of remains that would never be found.

Epilogue

"So, now you know," Snip said with a sigh. "The important parts, at least," Hex added. "The fall of our kingdom didn't come from a stolen love, like the rumors say. It came from our refusal to submit to death."

Snip leaned his head back against the rough stone and closed his eyes. "Unfortunately, death comes for us all and no matter what you try to do, you can't bring back the dead."

Their audience had listened intently, losing themselves in the story until their jaws went slack in disbelief and eyes wide in wonder and regret. All except Callen. Radnar's eyes flicked to the man, his hand clenching as he broke the silence. "You knew? This whole time?" he demanded.

Callen lifted a shoulder in a half-hearted shrug. "It was not my story to tell. And time does strange things to a memory. I barely recognized them."

"You should have said something when you realized who they were!"

"What would it have changed?"

Radnar flushed in anger. "We would have known the truth. We would have held our judgements and treated them better."

Callen arched a brow. "Why did you have to pass judgement in the first place?"

"Got you there," Snip chuckled.

Radnar turned from Callen to glare at Ryan. "And you!"

Ryan's eyes widened. "Me? What about me? What did I do? It's Callen you're mad at."

"You are Orion? *The* Orion? The son of Reaper, death himself. You knew what was going to happen, and you said nothing!"

Ryan's eyes darkened as he stood. "Contrary to popular belief, I cannot share what I see. I can only aid in ways that the Fates allow and, if memory serves, I told all of you to *stop keeping secrets*."

"That is not the point, boy," Radnar snapped.

"Yeah, well, they waged a war and brought down their entire kingdom by playing a chess match," Ryan countered.

Snip looked at his friend with betrayal lining his face. "Seriously?"

Ryan shrugged and mouthed "sorry" as Radnar whirled back to face the twins.

Hex's eyes darkened under Radnar's accusatory tone. "Grief twists your mind and darkens your soul. Everyone deals with it differently."

"And slaughtering your kingdom was yours?" Radnar asked.

Snip shrugged. "Some do as you did and drown themselves in drink or hide away like Callen. We choose a more proactive route and made everyone feel just a sliver of what we did."

"That is insane!"

"Yes," Hex agreed.

"Then why don't you—"

The walls shook under a sudden, vicious assault. Metal scraped stone, and magic hissed through the air as each armed themselves. Holding their breath, they watched the door tremble and Callen's stone barrier crack and break away.

The shaking stopped, and the doorknob turned ever so slowly. They tensed, poised to defend themselves, as the door cracked open. A hand wrapped around the frame, and two heads slipped through the opening.

Shock and disbelief washed over the room with the delicacy of a tsunami.

"Hey guys, we've been looking for you everywhere!"

Book Club Discussion Questions

1. What did you think of Hex and Snip's beginning?

2. What would you do if you were in Caelum and Evelyn's position?

3. How would you have dealt with the other Kings' demands?

4. Did any part of the book linger with you?

5. Do you want to know more about Hex and Snip? If so, what?

6. Did you race to the end, or was it more of a slow read?

7. Which characters did you like most? Which ones did you like least?

8. What do you think of Hex and Snip's punishment?

9. Do you want to know more about the punishment of Time? If so, what do you think it really is?

10. What would you say to Hex or Snip if you saw them?

About the Author

C.R. Rice is a fantasy/sci-fi writer, currently immersing you in the Realm Series. As someone who grew up in a small town, she has always loved escaping into the world of fantasy, paranormal and legend. C.R. has dedicated herself to creating that same opportunity for anyone who wants to escape the boring reality of real life. Through the years, she has traveled to dozens of different states and countries, has lived in North Carolina, Pennsylvania and now Florida! While they all have their own unique treasures, she admits to favoring the sunny southern states over the chilly northern ones, though there is nothing like curling up with a wonderful book by the fire as the snow falls outside the window.

Some of her favorite reads are Terry Pratchett's Disc World series, The Uglies Series by Scott Westerfeld, and The Hallow Kingdom by Clare B.

Dunkle. When she is not reading or writing, she enjoys spending time with her husband by the pool.

CPSIA information can be obtained
at www.ICGtesting.com
Printed in the USA
JSHW020906210323
39228JS00002B/155